Of Heritage & Heart
Story and Illustrations
by CLAIRE CARR

A limited edition
of 1,000 of which
this is number __*800*__.

WYNSHIP ARTS—1994

OF
Heritage
& Heart

Enjoy the adventure!

Claire Carr

OF Heritage & Heart

Story and Illustrations

by

Claire Carr

WYNSHIP ARTS
SAN DIEGO

First Edition
Library of Congress Catalog Number 94-60316
Copyright © 1994 by Claire Carr
All rights reserved

WYNSHIP ARTS
Claire Carr
4119 Legends Way
Maryville, TN 37801   ;52

Manufactured in the United States of America

ISBN 0-9640522-0-2

The paper used in this publication meets the minimum
requirements of the American National Standard for Information Sciences—Permanence of Paper for Printed
Library Materials, ANSI Z39-48-1984.

CONTENTS

Preface ix
Acknowledgements xi
1. Trail to Freedom 1
2. Missing 17
3. Survival 25
4. Echoes of the Past 41
5. Will McCalister 61
6. Feelings Within 79
7. Invisible Connectors 89
8. Coyote Call 107
9. Nature's Dictate 123
10. Yearnings 133
11. Encounters 145
12. The Birth 163
13. A New Home 175
14. The Visit 187
15. The Pack 195
16. Real Danger 209
17. Little Visitors 227
18. Good-By 237
19. Building Trust 245

20. Rescue 257
21. Hope 273
22. Silver Communicator 281
23. Peace 297

Waseeka's Bismark lumbered out of the back seat of the car with his human's permission. I remember standing transfixed as he ambled toward me, wagging his tail in rhythm to his gait. One could sense his totally trusting nature as he sniffed his "hello" and obediently responded to a quiet command from the young woman that he accompanied on his visit to my parents' home. He was marvelous! Never, from that day forward, has there ever been any other type of dog that I wished to share my life with.

Fourteen years later, in 1965, my husband gave me a gift—a little girl Newfoundland puppy. There has been at least one in my life ever since.

When we moved from the Midwest to southern California in 1978, four Newfoundlands came with us. A few months after we arrived, when I went out to feed the crew early one morning, the two youngest ones were nowhere in sight.

During the next four and a half days, I believe I lived the most difficult moments of my life. Not knowing.

The adventures depicted in *Of Heritage and Heart* are a product of my very active imagination in the face of fear, hope, depression, anxiety, and hope again. They are also an accumulation of real-life observations and experienes with my Newfoundlands. Writing the story was a way to clear my soul of a very heavy load.

Canine behavior fascinates me. Most of what is written into the story, I have seen happen. In the chapters of this book I have tried to draw together all those qualities I have lived with for nearly three decades and provide the reader with a clear account of the marvels of the spirit of the Newfoundland dog.

My dogs and I have thoroughly enjoyed our years in southern California. The chaparral country is beautiful and inspiring to me, and has offered countless hours of adventure for our dogs. A few non-dog drawings within these pages are presented for your enjoyment. They represent a fragrant and fascinating land like no other in the United States.

ACKNOWLEDGEMENTS

The river of life transports us through many fascinating adventures. Some we travel alone, but more often others are involved. I never cease to wonder at the impact one human can have upon another. At just the perfect moment, each of the following individuals came into my life to lend their expertise and encouragement. I am deeply grateful for each relationship, as for a time, the rivers of our lives were joined.

I wish to take time here to thank each person for his or her unique gift to me.

My husband, John, who provided the climate and encouragement to make this project a reality. And to our children, Charleen, JoAnn, Cheryl and John who grew up with Shipway's Avalon Holly, Am. Can. UDT. WRD., and Am. Can. Ch. Shipway's Knight Patrol, Am. Can. UDT. WRD. Together, they set the scene for much that I have come to understand and appreciate of the spirit that is the Newfoundland dog.

In the early 1950s, Ann Fee Elliott, long before she became my brother's wife, introduced me to her Newfoundland dog, Waseeka's Bismark. Many years later she willingly shared her literary skills and lifelong association with Newfoundland dogs to help me know what to delete from the original crudely done manuscript and gave the story its first coat of possibility.

Jude Rice volunteered to help with the first complete rewrite and put the manuscript on computer disc. Her ongoing love for Newfoundland dogs gave her a clear understanding of what I was trying to say.

Judi Adler is an expert on many phases of Newfoundland behavior and ability. Patiently, she worked with me on the early manuscript, challenging my meaning and intent where she found description or experience that did not seem in keeping with her understanding of breed behavior.

Stephen Reeve Blake, Jr. DVM, was my employer for a decade. He took time from his very busy practice to review the medical validity of the accounts in the book.

Dr. Dennis Fetko, PhD, known to many as "Doctor Dog," willingly accepted the challenge of reviewing the manuscript for accuracy of animal behavior, for that is his area of expertise, and he is ultimately well qualified. I am truly honored that he would do this for me.

Mark Martin appeared at a low point in my creative life. With just a few words he fired me with enthusiasm to finish what I had begun. He shared his knowledge of vital details important to proper preparation and presentation of a final manuscript. He, too, shares with me the love of the Newfoundland dog.

Sandra Millers Younger is a journalist who edited the manuscript for me. She reappeared in my life at just the right moment. I am indebted to her for her genuine willingness to share in this project. Her heart, too, has been captured by the Newfoundland dog. Her expertise was invaluable. Without her good-natured contribution I could not have completed this endeavor.

Seaworthy Trinity Bay CDX. WRD. TDD, my little girl Newfoundland, spent countless hours of the last rewrite of this manuscript lying nearby while I was at work on the computer. Her presence was necessary; her quiet patience was truly remarkable.

Of Heritage and Heart is dedicated to
every man, woman and child whose heart has ever
been touched by the spirit of a Newfoundland dog.

COULTER PINE

TRAIL TO FREEDOM

Wyn stirred, roused from a deep sleep by the throaty call of a nearby frog. She flexed her legs and shifted position, drew in a deep breath of clean winter air, then sighed and drifted again into slumber. Once more, the frog chirruped. It was an amazingly powerful call, which seemed as if it was intended to urge the big, black dog into wakefulness. But she slept on.

The night air drifted easily over Wyn's deep muzzle and played through her whiskers. Cool and moist, it teased her with familiar fragrances. The pungent odors of eucalyptus trees, evergreens, and primrose blossoms swirled about her as she drowsed. It was a pleasantly satisfying sensation, much like a gentle human hand stroking her softly.

From a far distance, a sound drifted through the blackness and across the southern California canyons. Again and again, the eerie serenade penetrated Wyn's

PACIFIC TREEFROG

sleep, finally bringing her to full attention. Her senses sifted the darkness, searching for clues to the strange and beautiful call she often heard in the night.

It came again, now becoming a chorus of high-pitched, yipping voices. The improvised notes blended, ringing out as if in celebration. Tingling to the marrow of her bones, Wyn jumped down from her perch atop her sleeping shelter and moved lightly from one end of the run to the other. Her muzzle held high, she searched the darkness for clues to the strange night music. Suddenly, the voices fell silent. Wyn growled a protest and stood quietly for a long time, listening. But the sounds were gone.

The big dog whined and paced restlessly within her enclosure, then stood still again as her ears strained for another call from the distant creatures. But all she could hear was the chirping of a persistent cricket and an occasional announcement from the nearby frog. She whined again, objecting to being teased and abandoned, then she turned her attention to her surroundings. The cyclone fencing encompassing the gravel run stretched a full fifty feet, giving her ample room to move freely. On one side, the enclosure was bounded by a high bank; on the other, by a walkway and the house where Wyn's humans lived.

Wyn took a drink of water, more to quench restlessness than thirst, walked over to her sleeping friend, Happy, and nudged her repeatedly in an impatient invitation to play. Happy lifted her head sleepily in Wyn's direction. Muzzles met and tails wagged as slowly, she pulled herself to a sitting position, waited a moment, then stood. In one slow, steady motion, Happy flexed her back and lowered the front half of her body to the ground, forelegs outstretched. She savored each pleasurable moment of her long stretch, then shook herself vigorously.

Now fully awake, Happy squared off against Wyn in the darkness, ready to meet her challenge. Alert and eager, the two young friends tumbled, pounced and rolled in a spirited game of chase and wrestle. Their kennelmate, an elderly male, lifted his huge head in droopy-eyed observation, then nestled his muzzle between his paws and sighed his commentary on their youthful exuberance.

Wyn and Happy were half sisters. The older male was their sire. They had been playmates since puppyhood, when they were carefully selected as hopefuls for a breeding colony of Newfoundland dogs. Wyn came from a kennel in the West. She was specifically chosen for her intelligence, working ability, and physical soundness. Happy was selected for soundness and beauty, and had come from a kennel nearby. Under the watchful eye of their human, the two puppies grew up together on a Midwestern farm. Both dogs learned basic working techniques. They were encouraged to develop their skills in natural environments, and, with supervision, they were allowed to run free in the fields, woods, and streams near their home.

But three months ago, when they were nearly two years old, Happy and Wyn, along with the old male, had left their beautiful farm home forever. With their humans, they had journeyed many miles through the

4

plains, over the Rocky Mountains and the Sierra Nevada range, westward to the sea and their new home in southern California. There was no stress for them in the move; they adjusted easily, savoring the many exciting aspects of their new surroundings.

The nighttime play continued. Up on their hind legs, Wyn and Happy sparred in mock combat, using their front paws as both weapons and to maintain their distance. After a few moments, they dropped to a standing position again and separated. Wyn faded into the darkness, while Happy braced against the fence, anticipating Wyn's next move. Although six months younger than her spirited friend, Happy outclassed Wyn by twenty pounds and an inch at the shoulder. Even now, as Happy approached maturity, she could not coordinate her one hundred forty pounds to outmaneuver Wyn's greater strength and agility. Pressing against the fence, Happy lifted her body to gain advantage over her unseen attacker. As she rose, her shoulder flipped up the latch on the kennel gate. When she lowered slowly to the ground, the gate stood slightly ajar.

Still apart, the two dogs played a waiting game in the darkness. Wyn stood silent, unmoving. Impatient, Happy finally gave up her defensive position and moved toward the drinking water. She took only a few laps. As her head came up, she saw Wyn's body flying toward her through the darkness. It was a solid blow, sending both dogs tumbling against the gate and out into the freedom of the yard.

Both Wyn and Happy loved it here. There were trails to explore and banks to climb. Big trees and great tropical plants created perfect hiding places for their games.

And the soft grass, a welcome change from their gravel runs, provided a cool, green place to roll and stretch. Now, with more room to run and tumble, their game built in intensity. Facing one another, the two big dogs crouched and lowered their heads, tail wagging, tongues lolling gently, as each waited for a first move. At last, by some secret signal, they leapt simultaneously into friendly combat once more, then broke apart into the chase. Their hearts pounded, their chests heaved as their playful maneuvers became wilder and their attacks, fiercer.

Hidden behind a cluster of ferns and palms, Wyn waited eagerly for Happy to discover her. Acting on a sudden impulse, she whirled out onto a path behind her. With her young friend in pursuit, Wyn galloped along the trail to the back of the yard, through an opening in the fence, and into a eucalyptus grove that opened onto a row of homes bordering the neighborhood's edge. Suddenly, the two dogs were at the street. Immediately, their attitudes changed. Their game-playing was over now; they had a new motivation . . . to investigate everything they encountered as they moved quietly past house after house of sleeping people.

Both Wyn and Happy were natural tracking dogs. Now all of their natural scenting abilities welled up within them. With noses down, they searched out each enticing whiff of aroma. Suddenly, one dog veered off to investigate an inviting trail; her companion quickly followed. A rabbit or perhaps a cat had traveled here, leaving invisible, but positive evidence for curious noses. The two dogs knew this area well; they had often walked with their humans past these houses on their way to the hills nearby. Now, driven by a primeval force within, they wandered farther and farther from their kennel home and their sleeping human family. At the end of the street, their black bodies disappeared into the dark chaparral.

Wyn and Happy dashed joyfully up the canyon and down their favorite path, across a sandy creek bed flowing gently with cool water, runoff from recent winter rains. With noses to the ground, the companions charged on recklessly, up the first hill, over the familiar rocky trails. They knew every inch of this terrain. Here, freed from city leash laws and encouraged to run off their youthful energy, they had spent many lighthearted hours with their humans. Here, they enjoyed freedom without demands. Often, they had dashed off wildly into the chaparral after a zig-zagging jackrabbit, which inevitably disappeared into the dense brush. Then, they'd run back, cheerfully panting, eager for a pat before bounding off again on their great search.

Reveling in their new freedom, the two friends pressed on through the darkness. The fresh night air seemed to enhance every familiar smell, tantalizing canine curiosity and urging the dogs onward into the hills, where the strange night music played. This was the world of the coyote, and it was abundant with game . . . leaping, running, crawling, flying, living lures for curious dogs. Quickly, Happy and Wyn fell into practiced patterns of team searching. Each remained aware of the other's presence and movements. Each honored the other's sudden acknowledgement of the presence of game, then waited tensely for the discoverer to make her move.

Not until they had crossed the outer edge of familiar territory did Happy and Wyn stop circling and searching. Standing at the crest of a hill, sensing suddenly that she had never been here before, Wyn lifted her muzzle high to test the fragrant air.

Happy joined her, standing tall beside her friend. Younger and more placid, Happy had always been a follower. Though she often went off on her own to investigate, she accepted the dominance and leadership of the older dog. Now she waited eagerly for Wyn's next move. She had never known the freedom to hunt the canyons and slosh through streams to her full satisfaction. Here, quite suddenly, was complete freedom. It pulsated through her body with every heartbeat, invigorating and exciting.

The two dogs stood motionless for a long time. They were breathing heavily. Their muscles tensed and their nostrils took in every new scent. As the sky began to brighten, the mesa country grew barely visible to the west. Beyond lay the Pacific Ocean, still enshrouded in early morning coastal fog. To the east, the irregular pattern of endless, rolling chaparral lifted gently to rocky, rugged foothills and, beyond, the backdrop of the mighty mountains of the Cleveland National Forest. After a final parting glance toward the mesa country, Wyn started down the hill on a trail toward the mountains. Her young companion accepted her decision willingly. Traveling together into the new day, the two dogs left behind all they had known. In the reckless innocence of youth, they chose to begin new lives.

After only a few hours, Wyn and Happy had already traveled many miles. Trails crisscrossed the hills, making it easy to cover the ground quickly and effortlessly. Still driven by the sheer joy of freedom, the two friends trotted on together into the unknown, their breath streaming out in white clouds behind them. The trail's spongy terra cotta soil provided easy footing. In places, however, it gave way to rocky areas, forcing the dogs to move more slowly as they picked their way over smooth, round stones. The two moved steadily forward, though sometimes only their minds could see the trail through the brush ahead. Occasionally, one or both veered off to investigate an inviting smell in the sage and manzanita. After a time, they joined again, sometimes walking side by side for a while before breaking into an easy single file trot.

At the bottom of a canyon, Wyn and Happy found a flowing stream. They waded in and began to drink, feeling the pleasant coolness run down their throats and spread into empty stomachs. Lost in the water's spell, the two dogs flopped down in the gentle current. Cool water flowed over their backs and around their shoulders in a caress as kind as any human hand, and, at this moment, far more welcome. They had traveled a great distance; it felt good to rest. True to their heritage, Wyn and Happy were comfortable, lying here with the current gently drifting over them. It seemed, for the moment at least, to fulfill every need. It was a long time before either animal felt the desire to do more than move her head for an occasional lap of fresh water.

Finally, both dogs lifted their dripping bodies from

the water, waded ashore, and shook. Hind legs struggled for steady footing as the violent shaking rippled from nose to tail. Water sprayed for six feet in all directions, drenching nearby rocks and shrubs. With their coats now shining and barely damp, both felt as refreshed as they looked. Full of new energy, Wyn started to move again. She followed along the stream for a while, then crossed it and moved onto another trail, still heading east. Happy followed.

The two traveled on through the canyon's sparse shrubs, over soft carpets of grey-green lichen and moss still damp from the winter rains. In places, thin, green grass blades pierced brown clumps of last year's growth, fresh salad for many small creatures of the chaparral and now for Happy and Wyn, who delighted in the fresh flavor. The green carpet felt cool underfoot as the pair padded through the grassy areas toward a thicket of dense brush. Each dog could have picked her way through easily if she chose; there were many small paths leading into the area. But the path of least resistance seemed the best choice. Wyn and Happy instinctively skirted around the thicket's edge, accepting the detour as naturally as any wild creature.

Suddenly, both animals came to an abrupt halt, responding separately to the same stimulus: Scent. The strong scent of a warm animal. Fully alert, motionless except for quivering nostrils, each dog took in every trace of the odor. Wyn moved her head slightly in search of a better reconnaissance position. Slowly, cautiously, she stepped forward, one paw at a time. With each step, the scent grew stronger and stronger. Wyn continued to assess the unknown odor, yet she remained silent, resisting the natural urge to sneeze and clear the scent from her nose; any noise would sound an alert.

About ten feet ahead of Wyn, Happy stood in the full flow of the scent. She knew the tantalizing warm smell came from the thicket and that she and Wyn were downwind from the creature. She knew, too, what the scent was. Once before, with her humans, she had met this sort of animal, chased it and been reprimanded. Now, here it was again! This time there was no human to interfere. Quivering with anticipation and curiosity, the two companions instinctively and simultaneously charged into the thicket.

Bleating in surprise and terror, three California blacktailed deer burst from their bed in the thicket and fled in separate directions. Startled by the explosion, Wyn and Happy halted in surprise. Then each dashed after a disappearing deer, whose magnificent high leaps carried it quickly and gracefully out of danger. One shot up the hill. Another started out after him, then turned in panic, tracing a huge circle toward a far hillside beyond the canyon. Here she met the third, another doe. The two does stopped and looked around nervously for their companion. They breathed heavily and flinched at every noise. Eventually realizing all was still, they calmed a bit and began to evaluate their situation. Still in the canyon, Happy and Wyn rushed through the high brush where the deer had disappeared, but found no evidence and soon gave up the chase.

Wiser than the does, the buck knew this country and its vantage points. He knew also where his companions were; he stood high above them now, surveying the entire canyon. Far below, he saw the dogs that had so rudely invaded his thicket. He watched them circle and sniff, alert but unconcerned, knowing that they were no match for his speed and agility.

Happy and Wyn returned to the thicket and explored it thoroughly. Three depressions in the soft ground cover showed where the deer had been sleeping. The air was heavy with scent, but the deer were gone. Next time, the dogs would be more cautious. Next time, they would be wiser. As they busied themselves investigating the thicket, the buck left his vantage point and carefully picked his way down the slope and across the canyon floor. Then, in a carefree, stiff-legged sprint, he vaulted up the hillside to join his nervous does. Together, the three deer bounded away over the hill in search of a peaceful place to enjoy an early breakfast.

Finally, Wyn headed away from the thicket, picking up the trail left by the buck. Happy's keen nose followed for a few yards before losing the scent. Wyn searched the area again, applying natural persistence to practiced search techniques. In time she discovered a pattern. First, scent was strong, then faint, then strong again, then gone. Following this pattern, Wyn traced the buck's path to his vantage point. From here, she, too, could see the canyon below. There was no animal to be seen. As if by magic, the marvelous-smelling creatures had vanished. Both dogs panted heavily with excitement, unaware of how foolish their domesticated ways would appear to a wild predator.

The December sun shot its first rays over the rim of

the mountains, bringing light to the tops of the highest hills. Wyn stood atop the summit, welcoming the warm streams of light. There was an air of elegance about her. Her dark eyes hinted of intelligence, kindness, and courage. Soon, Happy joined her companion. They stood together for a moment, their black coats glistening in the sunlight, polished by their journey through the chaparral. Then, suddenly, in perfect unison, they turned again toward the mountains and trotted off, spirited, strong, and free.

MISSING

Ann stood at the open gateway to the kennel run with three breakfast pans stacked in her left hand. Disbelieving, she doublechecked the empty shelters and turned to look at the yard. Comprehension came slowly, but inescapably. The girls were gone!

Feeling a nudge against her elbow, Ann looked down. It was the big male, gently reminding her that he was ready for breakfast. "Where are they?" she asked him as she set down his pan.

With a sense of frustration more than deep concern, Ann refilled the male's water dish and returned to the house. As she put the two bowls of food on the kitchen counter, she met Chuck's eyes with a frown. "The girls are gone, and I'd better go looking for them before we have breakfast," she said.

She crossed the house to the front door and opened it, half expecting the two wanderers to charge in at a gallop. No dogs. A quick glance across to the neighbors' yards, then up and down the street, brought another flash of frustration.

Ann stood in the doorway and listened. Occasionally Wyn and Happy had escaped and wandered off to investigate their new neighborhood, and if they ventured too close to another dog's yard, they stirred canine complaints. No barking. "Bother," she thought, "I'll have to use the car."

The aroma of fresh-brewed coffee added to Ann's impatience with the errant females. She was missing her treasured first cup of coffee because of them. Picking up the car keys, Ann grimaced in frustration. Chuck smiled, his eyes twinkling, as he toasted her with his own first cup of coffee. "Good luck, and hurry back," he said.

Making mental apologies to neighbors still sleeping early on Sunday morning, Ann began her slow tour of the block with two short blasts on the car horn. That always got fast results. Both dogs loved to ride. Ann knew they could appear at any moment now, charging to the car for a chance to go touring. But nothing. Still, Ann knew her dogs' habits. She could predict which way they would go. Slowly, she made her way up the hill and around the corner, checking every yard as she passed, sounding occasional blasts on the horn along the way. At the end of the winding road, without results, she turned back toward her house. Maybe they had returned while she was searching. But no dogs were waiting at the front door.

With a growing sense of concern, Ann expanded the

area of her search to a mile's radius. She drove by a city park where Wyn and Happy loved to play. Still, the car horn brought no response. Sitting at the park alone, Ann began to realize a sense of emptiness. Her dogs were not there. She got out of her car and stood in the chill of the morning, listening, and a sudden shudder passed over her.

On her way home, Ann noticed a poster nailed to a school yard fence. Someone had lost a cat. The poster included a phone number and mentioned a reward. As she drove along the empty, winding streets, Ann realized that she was looking for possible places to post signs of her own. Did she really need to do that? Surely not. She dismissed the idea quickly.

Home again, Ann was reaching for the knob when the door opened. Chuck greeted her. "I heard the car. Did you find our roaming females?" As soon as he saw her face, Chuck knew the answer.

Shaking her head slowly in disbelief, Ann walked past him, through the house and out into the backyard. They didn't come back, she thought. They aren't here . . . The big male came over and pushed his weight against her as she stood quietly, sensing reality. His head moved under her hand, lifting it as he maneuvered for attention. He could offer nothing but his presence, yet Ann counted it a precious gift, especially at this moment. Her hand cupped around his big head and drew him closer to her. The old dog could feel her sigh. "Where . . . are . . . they?" she asked him softly. "What should we do?"

★ ★ ★ ★ ★

Both Ann and Chuck spent the rest of the day search-ing, talking with neighbors, and tacking up signs about the lost dogs. Wyn and Happy had become well-known around the neighborhood in the three months since their arrival. They were big; they were furry, and tail-wag-ging friendly. Adults admired them; children loved them.

That night, when they went to bed, Ann and Chuck left the yard gate open, still hopeful that all three dogs would be there in the morning. But when morning came, the two females had not returned. The couple ate breakfast in silence. After a comforting embrace and an "I'll call you," Chuck left for work. Immediately, Ann busied herself with new ideas to bring her dogs home. Yet, always grinding in the back of her mind were diffi-cult questions. Were they stolen? Were they hurt? Could they come home if they wanted to? There were no an-swers.

Ann called the local paper and placed an ad: LOST: TWO VERY LARGE BLACK SHAGGY DOGS. FE-MALE. VERY FRIENDLY. REWARD. But the ad would not begin until tomorrow! Another whole day to wait and wonder. Another day to live with a growing fear.

Phone calls to area veterinarians yielded no helpful information. Office staff, some cold and impersonal, said they would be happy to post a notice, but only one person offered a degree of comfort. "Most of the time dogs find their way home to their families," she said. "Generally within a couple of days."

Chuck called at noon. Ann could sense a note of genuine disappointment in his voice when he learned Happy and Wyn were still gone. Trying to sound positive, she told of the signs now in place and the contacts with the veterinarians.

That afternoon, with dwindling hope, Ann called the two area animal shelters. A rushed voice on the line said the only way to know if her dogs were there was to come to see for herself. She did. No Newfoundlands. At the second shelter, a tall Mexican man was selecting a dog for his son. He asked to see the pictures Ann held in her hand. "Ah, beautiful!", he exclaimed, "In Mexico, we would pay much for dogs like these." Handing the photos back, he added kindly, "I hope you find your dogs."

Ann could still hear the Mexican man's comments ringing in her mind as she turned into her driveway. Though he meant well, the man had given her search a finality that until now she had been unwilling to accept. For the first time, Ann allowed herself to think that maybe she would never see the dogs again. She inhaled a quick breath and closed her eyes; they filled with tears. Then she forced the awful idea out of her mind.

Another night passed. The ad appeared in the newspaper. There were very few responses. Callers were either curious people asking silly questions or others who had sighted dogs that were clearly not Newfoundlands. Then, a lady with excitement in her voice, called to report that she had seen a pair of dogs running along the edge of a golf course. Ann listened carefully. This story was credible. But the woman lived thirty miles away.

Still, perhaps someone had picked up the dogs and later let them loose. Ann took down the directions and drove to the area. The caller met her as planned, but when Ann showed her photos of Happy and Wyn, she slumped in despair.

"Oh, no," she said, shaking her head. "These are really big dogs. I've never seen a dog that big around here. . . . I'm so sorry."

Eventually there were no more calls. Each avenue of hope had become a dead end. One evening, when the time came to fix a meal for her Newfoundland, Ann stood at the back door and stared out blankly. "Where are you?" she whispered. "Where are you?" Chuck moved to her from across the room. His warm hands held her shoulders and drew her close. She looked up at him.

"It's been over two weeks . . . they didn't come back," Ann said, choking on the words. "They didn't come back." Her voice broke, and she leaned heavily against him, sobbing, "And the worst part . . . The worst part is not knowing. . . ."

SURVIVAL

Five days into their journey, Wyn and Happy gave up their playful independence for serious hunting. Wyn's ribs showed. Happy, too, had lost weight, although it was not so obvious through her heavier winter coat. Still, the two dogs' spirit of adventure drove them ahead.

They wandered on into rocky hill country crafted with rugged beauty. Gigantic boulders consumed the landscape. They were thrust upward from the earthen floor, in the violence of some long-ago age, split apart by time and climate. Now they were surrounded by a soft carpet of green and brown grasses. The creosote bushes and manzanita nestled together in natural arrangements among the boulders, some showcased against the broad, smooth face of a granite wall. Occasionally, the grey-green beauty of a prickly pear cactus punctuated the scene. Now, in the rainy season, its rounded leaves were swollen with the precious liquid that would sustain the plant during the dry summer months to come. All around were the marks of abundant wildlife: a worn gravel path into a rocky crevice, a tiny hole in a clump of grass roots.

Wyn and Happy found this craggy terrain much more difficult to cover than the chaparral near their home. The sun beamed hot on their backs, and they took frequent rest periods in the shade of shrubs. After a time, they moved on, muscle-sore and tender-footed, and driven by hunger.

Early in the afternoon, quite by accident, Happy came upon a mouse. Disoriented by the sudden appearance of the huge dog, the tiny creature attempted to hurtle itself to safety in a series of leaps and dashes, but each time found itself farther from the shelter of its home in the grass roots, with Happy close behind.

Finally, as the mouse threw itself into one last frantic dash for safety, the dog lunged, and the chase was over. Happy devoured her catch quickly, but its tiny body could not quell the hunger that gnawed within her.

Long before dark, Happy and Wyn began searching for a place to stop and rest. The trail meandered upward, farther into the rugged foothills. At one point, it widened onto a rock ledge which curved around the side of the hill. Aching with hunger and fatigue, Happy walked out onto the ledge ahead of Wyn. She moved slowly, head down, eyes blank, tongue lolling in and out with each breath. Finding a spot of shade partially protected by a clump of dense brush, she flopped down, too weary

26

PRICKLY PEAR CACTUS

to paw a cool bed in the soil. Almost immediately, she was asleep.

As leader of the pair, Wyn's natural instincts would not let her rest until she had assessed their surroundings. The rock ledge was twenty feet wide, fifty feet or more above the shrub and boulder country below. It was a good vantage point. For a long time, Wyn stood looking out over the hillside. Then, for a moment, she glanced back down the trail. Despite her hunger and weariness, she felt no need to return home. Her whole being still reveled in her independence. The protected corner looked so inviting. Wyn walked over and sniffed Happy in a silent expression of appreciation for her presence. She circled the little alcove behind the bushes, made a single, half-hearted attempt to scratch out a bed, and then, with a moan, crumpled onto the sandy ground and slept.

It was a fitful, restless sleep for both dogs. Digestive juices flowed, squeaked, and gurgled in their empty stomachs. Their muscles twitched in painful spasms. No amount of play and exercise in the hills near home could have conditioned them for this experience. Darkness came, and the pair slept on, oblivious to the sounds of the night creatures around them.

With the first light of morning, white fingers of fog moved in from the sea and slowly crept up the canyon, knitting a thick, swirling, gray blanket that consumed everything in its path. Soon, the moisture had completely enveloped the two sleeping dogs. During the night, their muscles had finally relaxed, and now they slept peacefully, unaware that morning had come. For a long time, there were no sounds, only an eerie quiet, and then the drip and splash of water as the heavy fog collected on the desert plants and ran off onto the ground.

Precious water, so much part of the Newfoundlands' heritage, now became their lullaby, a beautiful, gentle song that comforted them as they slept. Cloaked in the gleaming moisture, Happy and Wyn seemed transformed into a pair of silver mounds on the red earth. Gradually, tiny flecks of water collected into droplets that beaded on their coats like heavy silver pearls before trickling to the ground, pooling momentarily, and then soaking into the soil.

It was well into morning by now, but still the dense fog insulated the two dogs from the new day. Finally, Wyn woke, but she did not move or even open her eyes. She was simply awake, mentally rousing herself, sensing where she was and how she felt. Her empty stomach ached with hunger, and her sore muscles argued against moving. A swirling waft of air crossed her muzzle; it carried a delightful aroma. Forgetting her discomfort, Wyn came alert.

She and Happy had met many of the little animals in the past few days, but they had always easily outmaneuvered the hunters and then vanished down tiny holes, leaving nothing but a teasing aroma.

Again, the squirrel's scent drifted past Wyn. This time, the creature was so near she could hear it! Without moving, Wyn opened her eyes and focused on the scurrying little animal. She was plump and gray. Her fluffy tail was much longer than her body, and her tufted ears, tinged with a rust color, seemed larger than they really were. From her burrow at the base of the bush where Wyn had spent the night, the squirrel had instantly noticed the two huge forms lying still in the early light. But both dogs slept so soundly, and their moisture-covered bodies blended so smoothly into the gray morning that she foolishly accepted their presence without feeling endangered.

Within Wyn's mind and body, the intense desire for food rose to a peak. She was so hungry. Still, she did not move. Saliva drained out of her mouth and onto the ground as she anticipated her first meal in six days. Yet, she continued watching the busy young squirrel, learning the pattern of its activities. This one must not get away. The pool of saliva grew beneath Wyn's head. Her brown eyes followed the squirrel as it moved recklessly to a spot far from the entrance to its burrow. Finally, Wyn was ready to make her move. The squirrel was not watching her, absorbed instead with scratching at a clump of grass. Wyn tensed. Now!

The big dog gathered herself in one monumental effort. In her mind, her body fulfilled her commands swiftly and gracefully. It rose easily, moved quickly toward the prey. In reality, Wyn's tight, sore muscles could not respond to her will. She could not lift her body from the ground, coordinate her actions, and leap with speed and agility as she expected. Instead, she lurched forward in a great, stumbling lunge, crying out in pain as her forelegs gave way and her muzzle dug into the gravel. Agonized by her inability to control her body, Wyn watched as the squirrel darted out of sight.

She grunted in despair, then lay still. Her legs refused
to move. Her muzzle stung. She throbbed all over. Her
stomach still gurgled and ached with hunger.

Slowly and with a great deal of effort, Wyn pulled
forward with her front legs, forced her hind legs under
her, and pushed herself into a sitting position. Then,
painfully, she stood, drawing her hind legs close together to support her tottering body. Her head drooped
nearly to the ground; her tail curled under her belly; her
abdomen tensed rock-hard against the pain. Moisture
from the fog trickled down her face and dropped off the
end of her nose.

Wyn walked a few paces forward, salivating so heavily the liquid trailed onto the ground beneath her. Her
rib cage began to heave, and, in one violent action, her
stomach threw out all the foaming yellow fluid it had
generated to digest the squirrel. Wyn gagged and
coughed, then shook her head to rid herself of the bitter
fluid and turned away.

The flurry of activity stirred Happy from her sleep.
She watched quietly as Wyn moved about, yet there was
no communication between them. Wyn lay down again
and curled into a tight knot of hunger and pain. The gray
fog swirled about her gently. Her body was drained of
all energy, and she slept once more.

Happy was now fully awake. For a long time, she
watched Wyn's still form. Her muzzle lifted, searching
for a scent related to the scene she had witnessed. But
no answers came. She began to move, then realized any
motion was painful. When she turned her head, her neck
hurt. Her shoulders and legs ached, and it was impossible even to breathe deeply without discomfort in her

back and ribs. Slowly, deliberately, she began moving and stretching. Gradually, she gained enough control to lift herself to a sitting position. From here, she studied the ledge area again. She looked back at Wyn, waiting for some movement, but seemed patiently resigned to her sleeping friend's lack of response.

Happy stood up, took a few guarded steps, and then shook the droplets of gray fog from her coat. Instantly she was black and shining again. Her first steps were stiff and awkward, but at least her legs were under her command once more. As she moved about, her muscles loosened, and she relaxed. Quietly, she walked over to Wyn. Curious, and at the same time longing for a spirited companion, Happy sniffed Wyn's head, exploring the bitter odor around her mouth. The investigation tickled Wyn's whiskers. Her lips twitched, and she moved her head. Happy wagged her tail with pleasure and anticipation, but Wyn simply changed position and continued to sleep.

Happy stared out into the gray wall of moisture, then looked back at her sleeping companion. Touched for a moment with loneliness, she whined a soft complaint before lying down close to Wyn, her great paws outstretched, her gentle face turned in Wyn's direction. Patiently, she waited for her friend to wake.

Warm sun poured over the hill country. The gray blanket swirled and thinned into a wispy canopy. Gradually, patches of pastel blue appeared above. The sun's rays began to penetrate Happy's black coat. Still waiting for Wyn, she moved to a shady area, then moved again when the sun's rays found her.

Finally, sunlight crept into the area where Wyn lay sleeping. She uncurled, stretched full length on the ground, her ribby sides exposed to the warmth. Wyn had always enjoyed sunbathing, especially in a favorite grassy spot at home. Now the warm rays penetrated her sore muscles, soothing her misery. Wyn took a deep breath and exhaled. Her paws, then her back legs, began to move. Happy watched with expectation. At last, Wyn was awake. She raised her head and began to look around.

With a single tail wag and a throaty woof, Happy scrambled to her feet, moving quickly to greet her friend. Wyn stood slowly and shook, tentatively at first and then more vigorously. Her muscles had relaxed in the sun, and she felt much better. Muzzles touched, and tails wagged. Together, the two companions readied themselves to move on. Happy emptied herself. Wyn, the dominant one, hurried to sniff the area, then covered Happy's scent with her own, leaving a powerful message for any knowing creature that might pass by.

The late morning sun shone warm on Wyn as she looked back down the trail they had traveled. Still, she felt no need to turn toward home. It was the unknown way ahead that invited her attention. With a parting sniff at the little squirrel's doorway, she headed out again. The path was rugged and narrow, but Happy willingly tagged along in single file behind Wyn. Rested and refreshed, the two dogs moved slowly at first until their sore muscles loosened. Eventually, the soreness disappeared.

But their hunger did not. Hunting became their primary motivation. Scent, the promise of food, was everywhere in the moist air; evidence of squirrels, cottontails, and jackrabbits met them at every turn. Yet by late afternoon, the dogs had nothing to show for their efforts.

Happy seemed far more eager than Wyn to veer off into the brush to search for game. During one of her sojourns, she encountered a cottontail. The startled rabbit zig-zagged through the high grass and darted across the path in front of Wyn, who joined Happy in the chase. With hungry stomachs and good noses urging them on, the two friends joined forces. Either one or the other was able to track their potential dinner.

With two dogs on its trail, the rabbit totally lost its sense of direction. Twice, it sought refuge in the brush, but the hungry dogs quickly discovered it and routed it from its temporary safety. Then, again, the rabbit found a hiding place. Both dogs saw it disappear into the grass; they could smell it nearby.

Wyn and Happy stopped and stared at the grass clump where they had last seen the rabbit. Cautiously, Happy lifted a paw, poised for the attack, and waited. For a few moments both animals remained completely motionless. Then synchronized teamwork took over. Wyn charged into the grass, flushing the rabbit out in Happy's direction. Countering the rabbit's attempted escape with speed and precision, Happy pounced. A momentary scuffle, a whistling squeal, then silence. The prize was hers!

Happy stood looking at Wyn with surprise in her

eyes. The limp body of the cottontail hung swinging from her jaws. She actually had the rabbit! In the next moment, she realized she was in trouble. She and Wyn were no longer companions. They were two starving dogs, and one of them had food. Quickly, Happy swung away, turning her woolly rump to Wyn's face, but still watching the other dog closely. This was not the friendly game of keepaway the two had played so often with a rope or a ball in their grassy yard. This was not a game at all, but the serious business of survival. Wyn moved quickly around to one side of Happy, who immediately turned away again, clinging tightly to the rabbit. Repeatedly, Wyn moved, and Happy countered, turning her head only enough to keep a wary eye on Wyn, but at the same time protect the rabbit from attack.

Hunger welled up in Wyn. Her sense of self-preservation demanded that she have food, and there it was, dangling before her. She could see it and smell it. She must have it! A growl developed deep within Wyn's body. She tensed, crouching slightly, and raised her hackles from her shoulders to her rump. With her jaws parted slightly, her ears flattened against her head, she curled her lips, baring two rows of white teeth. With her head lowered she looked directly into Happy's eyes. Wyn demanded the rabbit. She wanted it, and she intended to have it. She was the dominant one, the supreme commander; the rabbit was hers by right.

Happy fully understood Wyn's threat, but refused to heed the warning. Instead, she clamped harder onto her warm prize and turned to meet Wyn with a muffled growl. Starvation played equally on her usually gentle and submissive personality. She would not release the only meal she'd had in days. It was hers!

Flaring at Happy's response, Wyn snarled a more serious warning. Her upper lip twitched as she moved a step closer to the meal she wanted so desperately. At no time would she accept such a challenge to her dominance, especially not now. Like a triggered spring, she leaped at Happy and clamped her teeth over the dangling rabbit. Jerking away in surprise, Happy felt the solid tug of Wyn's weight at the other end of the rabbit. Each, quite naturally, wanted it all. Muzzle to muzzle, the two dogs glared at each other, growling, each demanding something neither would give. Happy tugged backwards. Wyn lowered her body and pulled harder. She was powerful, determined, and crazed by her desire for food.

It was a standoff. One tugged; the other growled. Without ever breaking eye contact, the two dogs dragged each other over the rocks and through the shrubs, deadlocked in mutual determination. Suddenly, Wyn felt Happy relax for an instant. She pulled again, throwing Happy off balance. The younger dog went down, still tenacious in her hold on the cottontail. Wyn tugged harder and harder as her anger rose. With her body close to the ground, eyes locked on Happy, she threw all her strength into one mighty pull. The fragile prize separated. Happy relaxed as she pulled her share to her and watched, unconcerned, as Wyn lurched backwards and tumbled down and the steep slope, her half of the rabbit still clenched tightly in her teeth. Wyn came to a halt in a small cactus growing against a large boulder. With a yelp of pain, she released her portion of the rabbit. She chewed at her hind quarters where the cactus spines had punctured her, then got up and shook, trying to regain her dignity.

Wyn picked up the life-giving morsel, carried it to a comfortable place and lay down. She gave the rabbit a few precursory licks, and looked around for Happy. Satisfied there was no danger lurking, she began her meal in earnest. Wyn crunched away eagerly. Soon bones, fur, and all had disappeared. She sniffed the ground around her, checking for missed morsels, but found nothing. Then, with long deliberate strokes of her tongue, she washed her front legs again and again until she was satisfied no indication of the rabbit remained on her. Next, her supple tongue curled up and around her muzzle, washing her face. Then she stood. Thinking of Happy's share of the prize, she set out to look for more food.

But Happy's half of the rabbit had disappeared as fast as Wyn's. It felt good in her stomach. She sat, licking her jaws, and watched Wyn move up the hill toward her. The older dog walked up to Happy boldly and sniffed the area around her. Then she sniffed Happy's muzzle and explored the area where she had eaten. Finally satisfied the rabbit was gone, she walked back toward Happy, who still sat in passive observation. The inner communication between the two dogs was free of animosity. An initial air of uneasiness quickly disappeared. Each had met her urgent need for food. Their violence had subsided along with their hunger.

With their friendship still intact and their stomachs working comfortably, Happy and Wyn accepted the mutual need to continue the hunt. Slowly at first, then with greater commitment, they paired again in team hunting. Together they headed off. Charged with renewed vigor and enthusiasm, they threaded their way through the brush and boulders toward the mountains.

COTTONTAIL

FOUR

ECHOS OF THE PAST

Far in the distance, thunder rumbled, playing a re-sounding kettle drum solo. Reverberations tumbled softly through the black sky, then trailed away to complete silence. Occasional lightning flickered in the rolling, gray clouds. The thunder answered with a firm and commanding voice. Both dogs were sleeping at the base of a live oak tree, curled into tight circles against the approaching storm. They were accustomed to the quaking fury of Midwestern summer storms, when screaming winds pushed sheets of driving rain across the land. By comparison, this weather seemed hardly more than a midnight serenade, orchestrated without fury.

It began to rain. Water drops sifted through the heavy foliage above the sleeping Newfoundlands. Their oily coats insulated them from the chill night air and shed water as easily as any sea captain's slicker. A stream of water trickled into the soil basin that Happy had dug for

41

herself and began to fill her cozy bed. Pooling under her, the chill waters touched her warm skin, causing her to shift positions, and finally waking her. She got up slowly and shook, spraying water everywhere, then moved to higher ground. Still half asleep, Happy circled on buckling legs before lying down again, curling herself into a round heap to wait out the storm.

At its peak, the full intensity of the storm unleashed lightning bolts from whirling clouds. It lit the mountain side with a brief and eerie light. Bolts danced at random and occasionally in duet, as the sparkling columns momentarily joining earth and sky. Inevitable thunder exploded, a powerful testimony to the storm's magnitude. Yet neither Happy nor Wyn felt disturbed by the sounds in the dark sky.

Then, in a sudden crackling explosion, an intense flash of light attacked a nearby pine, riveting down the slender trunk and burrowing into a dead branch. Great sparks of light flashed out from the tree as the current ripped away pieces of the wood. Almost at the same instant, a violent thunderclap jolted both dogs to their feet. Thunder shook the ground and vibrated above and below and all around them. Instinctively, they fled into the darkness, away from their oak tree shelter.

In a few seconds, it was over. Wyn stopped running, turned around, and stood staunchly, lifting her voice to the sky in throaty defiance to the storm. The stormy heavens answered with pelting rain, more rumbling, and swirling wind. Wyn's outburst threaded through the night to Happy's ears. She, too, had run in panic from the violent sounds. But there was no place to hide!

The sound was everywhere. When she finally stopped running Wyn was not with her. Surrounded by wind and rain, she felt lost and disoriented until she heard Wyn's protest. Happy turned directly toward the sound of Wyn's bark, stood for a moment to get her bearings, then trotted confidently in the direction of her companion's voice. As she drew closer, she made a soft woofing sound in the blackness to announce her arrival.

Wyn recognized her and turned to meet her. Occasional flickers of lightning illuminated their brief greeting. Their natural communication was silent and strong as they met. Then together they searched for a suitable shelter, safe from explosive forces. Sharing a mutual need for close contact, they walked and trotted along with single-minded purpose—to find another refuge from the storm.

At last they found a perfect secluded niche—a big shrub with broad, sprawling branches curving to the ground. Wyn moved in first, crouching to get under the branches. Happy followed close behind, maneuvering carefully around Wyn's body, taking care not to step on her. When she found her spot, she circled and tamped the ground, pawing halfheartedly with one foot. At last her big body flopped to the ground, and she rested her head comfortably on Wyn's back.

In the distance, the thunder rumbled on and lightning teased the sky into occasional light, but all of the storm's fury was gone. Rain fell gently. As the dark clouds drifted over the mountains and on toward the desert, their dwindling noises lulled the two companions back into a second sleep.

★ ★ ★ ★ ★

Overhead, the sky was still gray with watery clouds, but Wyn came awake with the first light. She was rested and alert. She crept out from under the shrub, found a place not far down the slope to urinate, then climbed back up the hill and flopped down on the cool ground. She was not hungry, so there was no urgency to be up and on her way. She liked it here. She and Happy had been gone from home just over three weeks. Still, she delighted in her freedom.

Testing the cool morning air with her sensitive nose, Wyn drew in the visual and pungent qualities of the area. The aromas were varied: grasses, trees, game, soil, all freshened by the storm. It smelled so good to her. Wyn felt an urgent need to know all about her new territory. With the big boulder country, the chaparral and its arduous challenges behind them, Wyn and Happy had journeyed on into the back country. Here, altitude and terrain permitted grassy open lands dotted with occasional live oaks. Gentle valleys were strung with flowing streams and occasional stands of California Sycamores and evergreens.

The grassland had presented the two dogs with new challenges. Its changing habitat provided different wildlife species for their menu, requiring new hunting strategies. Yet, for the moment, they felt at ease with their lifestyle. The daily quest for nourishment suppressed thoughts of home and humans, and kept them on the move.

As the light increased, the black silhouettes of live

oak, sycamore and evergreen trees became visible. Across the valley, mountains rose against the morning sky. Juniper, pine and cedar trees sprang up among the rock outcroppings. Nearby, a pine spiked the air with special fragrance. The fresh odor stirred something deep within Wyn as she took in a breath. A feeling was forming, easy and comfortable. The swirling evergreen scent jostled loose an image buried in her mind. Somewhere, sometime, she had known another place like this one, with green grass and pine fragrance. It was a time of happiness and contentment.

Wyn's memory drifted back easily now to the towering blue spruce trees that graced the lawn of her farm home in the Midwest. She had spent many pleasant hours playing and resting in the welcome shade they provided on hot summer days. In winter she'd romped around them, chest-deep in fluffy snow. Wyn felt a tingle of pleasure as the vision of her farm home began to emerge. She shifted her position eagerly as though it would help bring the picture into better focus. Pine fragrance, a grassy lawn, a familiar old brick farm house with a screened porch—all came clearly into view now. Why did this memory stir her feelings? Why did she feel such intense anticipation? What was she waiting for?

Wyn sniffed again. Slowly and deliberately, she "tasted" the scent, taking short breaths to ease the air into her body. There it was again! That one particular scent. . . .

Wyn's misty visions dissolved suddenly as reality intruded with swift impact. There was a split-second of activity in the valley before her. Tensing, Wyn focused

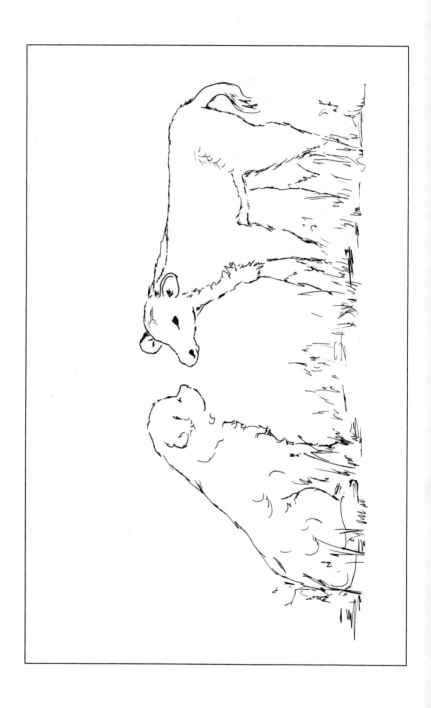

her attention now on the valley floor. Something was moving. It was enough to bring her to her feet. Ears alert for sound, watching intently for any new motion, she moved cautiously down the slope a few steps and stopped. Another flurry of activity! Wyn ran about forty yards toward the valley, then stopped again and remained motionless. Now she could see what had caught her attention, and it made her so happy that her tail wagged.

It was a young calf, a little female about a month old. Her young face gleamed white in the morning light. Knobby, white legs supported her strong brown body. Her colors matched perfectly the great mounds of pure-bred Herefords that surrounded her. Full of energy, the young heifer darted around the resting creatures, almost obscured by the tall field grass. Drawn by the exuberant activity, Wyn watched in amusement.

Just before daybreak, one of the cows got up, then ponderously ambled away from the herd. Not one of her company acknowledged her departure. None of the great heads turned as she moved away from the group. In recent weeks, each of the cows had taken her turn and quietly gone off from the herd. Like the others, nature now led this early riser to find a secluded spot for the birth of her calf. Before she returned, her newborn would stand, walk, nurse and learn discipline.

Wyn continued to watch the herd intently, moving closer as she did so. The scene before her was so familiar. All of her puppyhood had been spent around cattle, purebred Scotch Highland cattle. The shaggy beasts had grown accustomed to Wyn's puppy nose reaching into the feeding trough. She'd learned to be careful of the wide horns each Highlander carried, but she loved the sweet grain. She was always on hand and in the way, morning and evening at feeding time.

As she grew older, Wyn had often joined her human during calving. Although the cows were permitted to calve in the pasture, they were watched carefully. Usually someone was on hand to ensure that all was going well. Wyn's presence had been accepted by the laboring cows as long as she kept her distance.

Wyn was the only dog on the farm who amused herself by inventing games to play with the calves. She'd learned the adult cows didn't like to play, and it was best to stay away from the very young ones. But one- and two-month-old calves would romp with the nimble Newfoundland who was just about their size. As the calves grew older and their interests turned to mundane activities . . . grazing and chewing their cud . . . they lost interest in Wyn as a playmate.

On this chilly morning, Wyn stood as an observer, confronted once again with the pleasant possibility of a good romp with a familiar friend. She was close enough now to smell the cows. Warm and pleasant in her nostrils, the aroma stirred feelings that had lain dormant for many months. Bounding games of chase and frantic escapes from her farm playmates were always stimulating, challenging and fun. But her new home in southern California was in a city; there were no cattle, none of the excitement that was so much a part of her puppyhood. Suddenly, here it was again! For the first time in long months of comparative boredom, this chance meeting with the mountain herd was a welcome encounter indeed.

The calf persisted in her silly games. Still watching intently, Wyn again moved to close the distance between them. She sat quickly the moment she knew the calf had seen her. Wyn's big ears pulled forward in open curiosity, making her broad face look even wider. The calf studied the big, black thing in her pasture with a long, steady gaze. Then, cautiously, with single steps, she approached, sniffing the air, showing much more interest than fear. Wyn waited patiently.

The calf stopped and stretched her neck forward as far as possible, sniffing in Wyn's direction. The tip of Wyn's tail was wagging eagerly. Other than that she moved only her ears, but it was enough to make the calf flinch and draw back. Still curious, she came forward again, nearly touching Wyn this time. The big dog sat very still as her new young friend sniffed her carefully, snorted softly and sniffed some more. At last, Wyn came to her feet, tail wagging. The startled calf turned and fled in terror. The initial burst of speed took it about twenty feet; then it circled back and stood facing Wyn again. Curiosity and innocence overcame what fear the calf felt, and once more she closed the distance between herself and the large black dog. Their friendship seemed assured.

★ ★ ★ ★ ★

The screen door's squeaky hinge announced that the rancher was up and on his way again. He walked in long strides over to the corral where his gelding was nibbling the last few sprigs of hay from the dirt. The man lifted the latch on the gate, slipped through a narrow opening, then closed it securely behind them.

His presence drew a soft snicker from the pretty Appaloosa, and it moved toward him. Eagerly, the gelding presented his head for the bridle that was swinging from the man's shoulder. The rancher spoke to the horse in a deep, soft voice as he lifted the bit into place, slipped the leather straps over the big ears, one at a time, and secured the throat latch. Reins in hand, the rancher led his mount from the corral, across the open dirt area and back toward the house. The horse's shoes clicked on tiny pebbles in a pleasant rhythm as they walked. It was the only sound in the early morning. The rancher threw the reins over a tie rail by the front porch of his home.

There was just enough light to see by, but he could have saddled his mount easily in the dark if need be. He centered the saddle blanket on the horse's back and lifted the big saddle off the rail. With one swinging motion, it came to rest on the blanket. Swiftly, the rancher made all the necessary adjustments, talking to the horse all the time he worked. He checked the girth for proper fit around the horse, just snug enough but not too tight for his mount. At last, he lifted the reins from the railing, swung himself easily into the saddle, and reined the horse toward the dirt road that led up the mountain.

The rancher loved this early morning ride. Everything was fresh and clean with winter moisture. Rested and feeling good, he savored the cold air on his face. The gelding carried his rider at a fast walk. He, too, knew where they were going and needed no directions.

Ears pricked forward and alert, he showed his eager willingness to travel the trail. They made a comfortable team as they headed toward the quiet pasture to check on the prize herd of Herefords.

Now, there was just one more to be born, the rancher thought. This time the family could use a bull calf to feed out and eventually put meat on their table. Venison was easy to get and tasty. So were birds and rabbits, but nothing could equal good beef for a hearty meal. And he certainly couldn't butcher and eat any of those heifers! Jogging easily now, the horse and rider closed the distance to the sleeping Herefords. One more to go, he thought, in rhythm with his horse's gait, one more to go.

Just before he topped the rise overlooking the pasture, the cows' brawling protests reached his ears. His great fear was that the heifer was having trouble calving. His heart racing with the dread of impending disaster, he urged his horse to a lope that carried him quickly into full view of the herd. The cows were on their feet, each with a calf standing safely behind her. And there stood Wyn facing the multitude of worried mothers.

Taking in the entire scene in a moment, the rancher saw only a marauding dog attacking his herd. He reached behind the saddle and touched his rifle, just to reassure himself that it was there, then moved down the slope toward his prized animals. The fear of what he might find made him cold, then sick in the pit of his stomach. There were coyotes around, of course, but they didn't worry him. They wouldn't hurt a healthy herd. But this was a big dog, capable of doing a lot of harm.

The rancher's body flushed with anger. As the area's population increased, more arriving city families brought along one or two dogs and often turned them loose to run. Joining together in small packs, the roaming animals sometimes became killers and had done some real damage. Young cattle had been maimed so badly they had to be destroyed; chicken houses has been attacked and whole flocks ruined. A neighbor lost a barn full of sheep. Total havoc. Meaningless destruction. The ranchers had all agreed to shoot to kill in situations like this. Their valuable stock had to be protected. Besides, city folk had no business letting their dogs roam free. They were not allowed to in the city, and they shouldn't do it in the back country either.

The rancher's heart beat rapidly now as he drew within close range. A quick survey of the herd told him one cow was missing, the one due to calve soon. She was nowhere in sight. Seeing the Herefords on their feet facing the big black dog, anger welled up within him anew. He hated free-roaming dogs. He had never seen one like this around here before, but he knew it meant trouble for his herd. Moving deliberately, the rancher eased his horse to a halt and slowly reached for his rifle.

Wyn stood facing the half circle of bellowing, worried mothers. This was not the way it was on the farm. The cows there did not become agitated and nervous when she came to play. Sensing the other animals' intense fears, she began to develop a few of her own. This was not a safe place to be.

She turned away from the cows and angled toward the fence where she had entered the field. Suddenly, the movement of the horse and rider coming toward her caught her attention. She stopped and watched. This man was the first human she had seen in many weeks. It warmed her with happiness to see him coming toward her atop his big horse. She broke into a trot and headed directly for them, then stopped, her tail wagging gently as she stood watching the horseman ride slowly in her direction.

The rancher's eyes swept the pasture once more for the missing cow. Where was she? Which direction did she go? He must find her quickly in case there was a chance of saving her or the calf. He didn't want to think of her suffering. His heart pounded with fear and frustration as he visualized what the big dog must have done to the newborn and its mother. Life was so cruel. Why? Hate filled him. Why did that black devil have to come here now? Why?

The dog was already in easy range. He was one of the best shots on the mountain. He knew he would not miss. It struck him as odd that the big dog just stood there, looking at him with those demon eyes. He watched the animal confidently, taking advantage of his edge.

Wyn stood perfectly still as the horseman approached. Something was happening she did not understand. She could sense the man's emotions pouring out from him and spilling over her, announcing impending danger. Suddenly, Wyn felt an immediate and desperate need to escape from this man. Her longing for human contact and the joy of the encounter faded abruptly; now it was only fear that she felt. Her body quivered, but she seemed momentarily frozen in position, facing the rancher as he reined his horse to a stop. As he raised his rifle to his shoulder, she looked into his face. The fury in his eyes hit her like a hot iron. She must run now! She must flee for her life! Wyn wheeled in terror, her heart pounding with a fear she had never known. As she turned, the rancher fired.

The rifle report echoed back and forth across the valley. He had aimed straight for the heart and the big dog fell, tumbling to a stop, as he knew it would. He couldn't even see it in the tall brown grass. Nudging his horse toward the spot where he saw the dog fall, the man stopped and gazed down at the huge body in the grass. The gaping wound on the shoulder told him he had hit his mark. The dog's tongue lolled from its mouth, and the half-opened eyes had the look of death. The big dog was stilled.

All of the hatred left him now that he had vented his fury and settled the score. It was a female, he mused, as he looked down at the black carcass. What a big one, too! He leaned over in his saddle and poked at the still form with the barrel of his rifle. He wondered for a moment what kind of dog she was and where she'd come from. With one last glance down at the animal, he put his rifle back in its sheath and looked up across the valley toward his beloved Herefords. They were safe now. All but one. Where was that heifer? Was there a calf? He set out, the fear still gripping his heart, and never looked back.

The rifle shot brought Happy from the hill above the pasture where she had been hunting. She appeared just as the rancher rode out of the north end of the valley in search of the missing heifer.

Tracking Wyn was easy. The trail led down the hill, under the fence where a dry creek bed permitted easy access to the big field. The strong scent of horse and man now joined Wyn's trail and hung heavy in the air. She heard a sound and looked up, sniffing for more airborne clues. There was nothing visible, so she put her muzzle into the tall grass and searched on. She was moving fast when she came upon Wyn, who was still lying on her side, but whimpering now and shaking violently.

The bullet had struck her a glancing blow. She had turned just at the moment the rancher fired and thus missed the shot's full impact. Still, the bullet had ripped into her shoulder muscles and shattered part of her shoulder blade. Mercifully, her body's natural pain killers were at work protecting her from the full pain of the injury. Nothing, however, could relieve the fear that urged her to get up and away to a place where she could feel safe.

Happy did not understand how Wyn had been hurt, but she knew something was wrong. She sniffed her companion all over. A wide gash in her shoulder was bleeding. Wyn lifted her head in response to Happy's presence. As she regained consciousness, fear of the man overwhelmed her and she tried desperately, but in vain to get up. A driving imperative to run urged her to try again and again. Happy sensed her need to move, and her presence gave Wyn strength. Slowly, the injured dog pushed to a sitting position. It took nearly all of her strength to fight the shock of the shattered shoulder blade. She was wobbly but held her place and rested.

Wyn felt frightened and vulnerable. She looked around nervously. The man and the horse were gone. In the distance, she could see her brown and white Hereford playmate staring at her silently. Wyn's shoulder was seeping blood. But she must stay up. She must walk. She must keep moving. She took a few faltering steps, with Happy following close by her side. Looking for a safe place away from the cows, Wyn limped painfully toward the pine trees to the east. From somewhere deep within her, she felt a sudden rush of warmth and strength that consumed the hurt and fired her determination to escape. The urgent need drove her on toward the shelter of the mountains. As she moved, her fear began to leave her. The farther away from the pasture she got, the less anxiety she felt.

Wyn did not understand what had happened, why her gesture of friendliness has ended in overwhelming fear, but she could still feel the man's anger. With Happy by her side for protection, she forced her injured body to keep moving toward the rocky outcroppings of the mountain.

They stopped frequently to rest, and then moved on. Wyn's shoulder continued to bleed as she hobbled along toward safety. Her injured leg would not hold weight at all, but she managed to make her way on three legs. After a tortuous two-hour journey, the dogs found their refuge on the mountainside . . . a cave-like recess secluded and protected on three sides and large enough for both of them. Wyn could rest here. She stood precariously, holding her injured leg off the ground. By some miracle she'd made it to safety. Happy's presence had given her the strength she needed to flee from the danger. Here at last she felt secure; the desire to escape melted away. Weak and weary, she slowly maneuvered her body into a sitting position and then slid carefully to the ground.

Wyn felt secure within the recess of the ledge. She liked the leather-leaved shrubs that secluded her from the outside world. She tried to find an easy way to rest her throbbing leg and shoulder, but each new position placed stress on the injury. Almost as soon as she'd stopped traveling, however, the bleeding stopped. As long as she rested, healing could begin.

As soon as Wyn settled, Happy's curiosity drew her close enough for a sniffing examination of the wound. She tried to lick its crusted surfaces, but backed away when Wyn looked toward her and growled. Still puzzled, Happy lay down in silent speculation.

Wyn breathed a great sigh of exhaustion and relief. She felt safe here. She lay very still, sensing her peaceful surroundings. She became suddenly conscious of her wounded shoulder. She sniffed the area examining it carefully, then washed around the edges of the wound and tried to clean the blood from her shoulder and leg. But it was too painful, and she was too weary. Stretching out her head on the ledge, she relaxed her shoulder into the most comfortable position she could find and willingly gave herself to fitful sleep.

Winter sunlight flowed down over the mountains. It was mid-day. Evergreen trees towered overhead, emitting their special fragrance in the sun's warmth. In her restless sleep, the aroma of pine drifting about Wyn, once again triggered visions of cool green grass, a friendly farm home . . . of someplace far away. The misty visions came and went as she drifted in and out of sleep, troubled by fear and pain. Sweetly this time, Wyn's dreams came clearly into focus, penetrating her wafting consciousness. She saw the farm house . . . the screened porch . . . and a human. Then there was another home, this one sheltered by tropical plants. . . and a human . . . then green grass and pines, and again, the same human. This time the human had a face and gentle hands, and Wyn felt happy as in her dreams she romped and played with the human. The dream comforted her. This was the human she knew she could trust! And in her dreams, she expressed her joy with a wagging tail.

FIVE

WILL McCALISTER

The sound of Will McCalister's hammer echoed across the valley as he resolutely drove nails into the pine boards of the new gate. Each blow brought him closer to a finished project. The work helped to relieve the frustration he felt when he thought of the coyote and, even more, his anger at himself. He shouldn't have lost his old rooster. "I could have prevented it!" he thought out loud in rhythm with the pounding. "What made me think that I . . . could . . . not . . . miss! Never . . . again. . . will . . . that . . . thieving . . . coyote. . . ."

Will had tried to start his morning in the usual way. At dawn, he'd opened the heavy slab door of his cozy mountain cabin and walked out to the narrow, wooden porch that ran the full length of the east side. His pipe was packed carefully with his favorite tobacco. He put it between his teeth while he drew a match from his pocket. Soon, the smoke began to curl and eddy before him, drawn by the gentle currents of the morning air.

Maybe someday this pipe would become as comfortable as the "old friend" he'd lost out there on the trail. He drew again on his pipe. Some of the smoke drifted down and settled in his beard, its light and dark lines perfectly matching the gray patterns there. His hair was etched in grey. It blended with his beard, wreathing a kindly and weathered face.

The yapping call of a coyote stirred frustration within him. In the distance another responded with its frenzied song. Will listened and remembered. This was the third day since that thieving coyote had stolen his prize rooster. Maybe that yipping creature was the very one he had chased through the darkening forest. Maybe that was the one that caused him to lose his pipe. The irreverent morning yodeling came again, and again. Will wondered if it was the villain's voice. It sounded like a male. It wasn't very far away. Will puffed on his new pipe and felt resentment toward the coyotes as he watched the smoke curl and drift gently on the morning air. He thought about yesterday. He hadn't really minded the trip down to the store. He needed supplies. And the pipe would eventually lose its newness and feel a bit more like his old favorite. The only problems he had to deal with now were replacing the old rooster and fixing the hen house and yard to make them coyote proof. He puffed with conviction now. Yes sir, that coyote had tasted its last free meal from this hen house!

Will finished his smoke and tapped the pipe barrel against the side of the porch railing as the sun was coming up. He made mental notes of the tools he needed

BED ROCK MORTARS

for the repairs. He liked the sunny days of winter. The crisp air invigorated him; he preferred cold and occasionally snow to the searing hot days of summer on the mountain.

Will went into the cabin and placed the pipe on the scrubbed wooden mantle where he stored his tobacco. He washed his breakfast dishes with water warmed on the tiny wood stove, pouring hot water over the plates, bowl and cup. He lifted the little pan of steaming rinse water and tipped it to drain every silvery drop over the clean utensils. He wiped the cast iron skillet in circular motions, studying the glossy results as he worked. He never washed the favored relic; just wiped it thoroughly to remove all greasy residue.

Will turned from the sink, tucked the skillet away on a low cupboard shelf, and glanced around the room. It was pleasant, especially with the sun streaming in. The bed was tidy, all its covers in place, the brightly colored quilt splashed with sunlight. His cozy home was one big room, very economically heated by the little wood stove, or the fireplace with its generous hearth. He looked forward to the fire that would burn there in the evening when his day's work was over. The kindling and split logs were in place and ready to light when he came in for his evening meal. Will was happy here.

"Okay, you bandit," he said with a sense of challenge in his voice, "We'll see what we can do about you." Will opened the rough-board gateway to his porch, took the steps two at a time, and with confident strides, headed for the tool shed. Deliberately, he selected each item: the proper hammer and nails of course, his saw, and the homemade fence stretcher, skillfully crafted with ropes and old pulleys. He estimated he had just enough fencing to bar the culprit from another free meal. Finally, Will collected his new lumber, two by twos and a section of two by four, then another, just to be sure. He assembled the gear carefully in his left hand, balancing the weight as he tucked the lumber under his big arm. He headed for the chicken house, his determination tempered by a bit of humor. It was his turn now. His opponent . . . the coyote.

Will dropped the tools near the scene of the crime, a clearly visible area where the coyote had torn at the fence with his teeth and nails to gain silent entry. The chickens were still confined within the shelter. As Will entered their domain, the hens greeted him with their usual clucking expectancy. He scooped their morning ration of grain from a large bag with a pan and scattered it by hand it on the ground.

The chickens pecked and scratched and occasionally scuffled over a single kernel as they hurried to fill their craws. Never in all his years of raising chickens did Will feel that they really trusted him. They cocked their heads up at him with a wry, one-sided stare, their red-rimmed eyes showing no emotion. It always made him feel a bit uneasy, as though they knew his stew pot was their eventual destiny.

Caring for the chickens was a necessary chore, but repairing the fence was a challenge. Will had set to work joyfully on his hen house repair, and the project was going well. At last, the final nail driven, the gate was complete. He leaned it against the fence and stood back to admire his work. "Now, Mr. Coyote," he said through a grin. "Try this one!" With new fencing material in hand, he next set out to secure the enclosure, measuring his skill and knowledge against an animal he judged to be very clever.

★ ★ ★ ★ ★

The coyote voices had stirred other creatures on the mountain. From her refuge, Wyn could hear them clearly. The dogs had been secluded there for four days now, and this was the first time that Wyn had indicated she cared about the presence of coyotes. This morning, her hackles bristled at the call, the same sound that had awakened her from sleep in her kennel. Wyn had no reason to react that way to the odd canine communication. She had heard it many times since she came to live in California, yet it stirred her now as it did then. She growled, low, muffled, almost inaudible, but it was enough to rouse Happy.

Responding to Wyn's warning, Happy jumped to her feet to stand guard. Lifting her head, she sniffed and listened. No more sounds. No alien scents. She could find nothing in the forest to concern her. Finally she shook, releasing her tension, and walked over to Wyn. Greeting her injured friend, Happy breathed lightly over Wyn's eyes and ears in a friendly gesture. Then her muzzle moved down to the gaping wound on Wyn's shoulder. She washed it gently as if she understood that it was painful and hoped she could offer a measure of comfort.

Satisfied that Wyn was safe, Happy left the ledge and

headed out to get water. She could find it easily during the rainy season. Indian grinding stones were plentiful in the area and collected water after each shower. The big dog lapped eagerly, feeling the cold water spreading from her throat down into her empty stomach. It was time to go hunting. Although it was more difficult to hunt alone, it was not impossible. Happy continued to find plenty to eat and frequently brought kills home to the ledge for Wyn, who showed little interest in food.

As her body healed, Wyn slept most of the time, moving only enough to change positions in an effort to be comfortable. The searing, sharp pain in her shoulder was subsiding, but the unrelenting soreness was a constant reminder that she could not be active. The bleeding had stopped, replaced by clear fluids that seeped continually. It was still a very nasty wound.

Although it was impossible to put any weight on the injured leg, Wyn was well enough to respond to the basic needs. Two or three times a day she got up and made her way to a nearby pool of water to drink and to empty herself.

Her sleep was still haunted by memories of the menacing form that caused her pain, but other dreams of peaceful times with her human mixed in with the fearful images. Often she awakened feeling hurt, confused, and lonely. Now, on this fourth day after the shooting, she was more alert. For the first time she began to feel twinges of hunger.

Wyn washed her injured shoulder as best she could, responding to her need to keep the wound clean. She raised her head, hoping to catch a scent of Happy, whose early morning hunt had left Wyn alone on the ledge. She waited now with anticipation.

With her own hunger temporarily abated, Happy continued hunting until one unwary cottontail became her food gift for Wyn. Dedicated to her duty, she hurried to the ledge with the rabbit clenched tightly in her jaws, swinging in rhythm to her footsteps. She trotted around the ledge and stood proudly before her companion, head up, tail waving slowly, clearly indicating pleasure at her accomplishment. Slowly, she lowered her head and deposited the gift well within reach of the injured dog. Happy watched for a moment. As Wyn began to show interest. Happy backed away from her and returned to the forest to pursue her own needs.

The rabbit's warm aroma intensified Wyn's hunger. She sniffed toward the carcass, then stretched her neck forward, gently took hold of Happy's offering, and drew it to her. Deliberately at first, and then with growing interest she tended her prize, as if it took time to recall how to eat. She sniffed and licked the furry form, moved it about with her nose, then licked it some more. Saliva flowed from her mouth and drizzled over the rabbit. For the first time in days, Wyn felt strong and alive . . . and hungry. She devoured all of her breakfast.

For the next ten days, Happy continued to bring food to her healing friend. Improvement was rapid. It became quite a task to search out enough food for herself and meet Wyn's growing appetite as well.

★ ★ ★ ★ ★

Hunger hurried Happy along to an area where she

knew game was abundant. Her nose checked randomly along the way. Suddenly, she came upon a scent that intrigued her. She stopped abruptly and circled to examine it more carefully. It was a mixture of things: chickens for one, like those she used to chase as a pup on the farm. The smell of blood combined with the familiar scent of coyote, left an invisible account of a recent kill. But the scent that drew Happy forward and made her tail wag with pleasure was human. It was a three-day-old scent, but the human odor was so distinct from the usual creature scents of the forest, it required little effort for her to follow.

The human scent spawned deep feelings. As she snuffled along searching for the intermittent odor of man, the memory of her life with humans, her need to be touched and stroked by a human hand, quickly overpowered her need for food and her duty to Wyn. Compelled by this need and her natural hunting instincts, she pushed forward, trotting when she was sure of the direction, or walking, nose down, as she searched for each clue that still clung to grass or gravel. Occasionally, so many odors mingled that Happy had to sneeze and clear her scent cells. Then she renewed her search for the human scent that she knew would lead her to her target.

There were deep footprints in the moist areas of the trail. Happy found the compelling scent strongest there. She stopped long enough to sniff each print thoroughly, inhaling the invisible clues. As she mulled over the footprints, the wonderful human scent intensified her desire. She must follow. She must find the human who left this trail. A feeling of loneliness became her motivation.

The search led her to the edge of a clearing. There before her stood a small cabin and other small buildings. She could hear the familiar sound of clucking chickens. No dog barked to warn of her arrival, but she heard a human voice, humming a tune, and the rhythmic pounding of a hammer.

Happy had no thought in her to be cautious. She walked forward boldly. The morning breeze wafted gently in her direction, carrying Will's scent, inviting her to come closer. She broke into a trot, heading directly toward the man. He was bent over, his back to her, intently working on the door frame of the chicken house. Happy rushed up to him, thrust her huge head up under his arm and greeted him with such force that he toppled sideways to the ground. Immediately she was on top of him, licking his face and walking over him with joyous exuberance.

Will was terrified. He couldn't breathe, yet he knew he wasn't hurt. It wasn't a bear. That had been his first fear. He collected himself as soon as he realized that whatever it was, it was friendly. Will was strong and able to maneuver with a great deal of agility. He quickly rolled over and bounced to his feet, then faced his assailant, a piece of board in his hand. "My God," he whispered as soon as he saw her. "It's a dog! The biggest dog I ever saw!" he thought to himself. The animal certainly appeared pleased to see him. He was relieved it looked so friendly, especially since it was so big. Will let the two by two slide from his hand to the ground, and stood for a few moments studying the animal. Then he gathered his breath and without moving spoke softly to the dog.

Happy wagged her tail widely from side to side. Her ears stood alert as she looked at him with an eager, expectant expression. She sidled up next to him, waiting for the scratching and patting she she would receive from the human.

Will realized quickly that the big animal presented no danger. His hands fell to her naturally, stroking lightly at first, then with more vigor. Amazement welled up within him as he felt the dog's size and power. It was a female.

Will sighed heavily. His shoulders slumped in relief as he realized how much tension and fear had gripped him in the first moments of the big dog's surprise visit. Feeling his knees go weak, he sat down in the dirt.

Happy rolled down on the ground next to him, belly up, with a pawing demand for him to continue the stroking. This was the human contact she missed. This was the need that had lured her from Wyn and her own breakfast. She could feel this man's gentle nature as surely as he could sense the same in her. They became instant friends.

The man and the dog spent a half an hour or so together there, each for separate reasons. Will's curiosity about his visitor grew as he thought more about her. She was quietly demanding, and he was a willing subject. Urged on by her big paw, he continued to stroke her as she continued to savor long-forgotten feelings of pleasure and comfort. Will was amused, then intrigued by her ability to communicate her pleasant personality and her wishes. He was amused at himself even more, sitting there in the sun as though his day's work was over. Slipping back into reality, he massaged her big body and neck vigorously with both hands, then broke the silence. "Well, big girl, I have a job to finish," he said in his deep and gentle voice. With a final pat to Happy's woolly head, he stood up, brushed the soil and pine needles from his clothes, picked up the hammer where it had fallen during their encounter, and went to work again on the door frame.

Will's curiosity about the big dog grew as he thought more about her. How had she come to be here on his mountain? He decided she must belong to one of the newer families that had moved into the mountains from the cities. He'd ask around the next time he went down to the store. Now, maybe she'd like a drink. So he made a special trip to the cabin to find a suitable water pan for his visitor. He reached for one, stored under the sink, handled it pensively, and then, smiling, tucked it back in the stack and drew out the very large one. Returning to the yard, he headed for the water pump.

She didn't look hungry. No, he was sure she wasn't hungry, except for affection. Will patted her again, and set the pan of cool water in the shade for her. Turning back to his hammering, he began explaining to her about the problem he'd had with coyotes and chickens.

It had been a long time since there had been a dog on the place. Will thought about it as he worked. With a dog around, likely as not, the coyotes wouldn't bother his chickens. She's sure big enough to handle herself, even against a coyote, Will thought. The thick coat would protect her if there was a squabble. He wondered if she would stay around. She did seem to like him.

Maybe if he shared his supper with her it would serve as an inducement. "Yes," he thought, "he really would like to keep that dog around." She wore no collar, and there was no hint that she ever had. He didn't like to tie up a dog, not up here on the mountain. She needed to be free just like the wild creatures of the forest. Whenever Will had seen dogs tied up, it made him hurt for them, for he could see their whole, sad existence tethered to a rope or a chain, anchored to a doghouse that allowed only enough freedom to run a circle in the dirt, offering nothing but frustration and loneliness. No, he wouldn't tie up this pretty dog, but he would feed her and hope she would stay.

All day long, Happy served as Will's constant companion, listening intently to his running stream of conversation. He finished the chicken house, repaired a tire on his wheelbarrow, then fixed a small leak in the porch roof over the wood pile. That evening, Happy received a generous portion of supper. She accepted it readily, licked her chops, and, with black eyes looking deep into his, clearly asked for more. "Will," he thought to himself, "that dog will eat you out of house and home!" Then he offered her a large chunk of homemade sourdough bread for dessert.

As evening approached, Happy joined Will for his evening smoke. Spreading herself out on the tiny porch, she made it look even smaller. It was so satisfying to be near a human again. An overwhelming feeling of contentment filled her as she relaxed with him. She watched intently as he lit his pipe and puffed away.

Will spent a few minutes watching the smoke ebb and

flow in its beautiful patterns. Then his gaze traveled far beyond to the orange and purple of the mountains in the evening light. Finally, his attention came back to his big companion. To him, it was an intriguing feeling to have company.

It had been many years since Will had lost his lovely bride. The falling tree . . . The feelings of desperation and helplessness temporarily returned . . . painful memories of that awful day. Time had taken away the pain. He decided to stay here on the mountain instead of returning to the lumber business he knew in northern California, because it was here, on the mountain, that he was happy. This had been their home, and now it was his home. Loneliness rarely plagued him anymore. But now, there was another living being here beside him . . . and that was a good feeling.

The tobacco embers burned low; Will's reverie with his pipe was over. From where he sat on the railing he leaned over and tapped out the black ashes onto the ground. He sat still for a long time in the gathering dusk. Once, the big dog got up and came to him. He reached out and stroked the top of her head. When her need was met, she turned and ambled slowly over to the spot she had selected by the wood pile and flopped down with such force that it dislodged a gasping sigh from her throat and vibrated the boards under Will's feet. He smiled. He could sense that she was content. In the gathering darkness both man and animal felt it was good to have one another.

Drowsiness came over Will. The mountains were quiet. A coyote called faintly in the distance. Will walked over to the big dog. She was sleeping soundly now, stretched out full-length with her back against the wall of fire wood. He bent down and ran his hand over her head, stroked her neck and down her rib cage, along her side and over her rump.

As Will climbed into his bed that night, he was acutely aware of not being alone. He thought of the great bear-like creature asleep outside the door. He knew that she would be there to greet him in the morning, and he was glad.

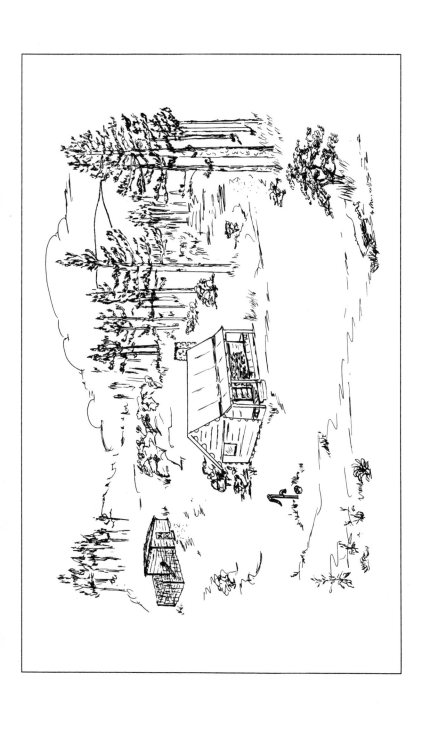

SIX

FEELINGS WITHIN

The sounds of morning reached Wyn's ears. She awakened easily. Lifting her head, she looked about, studying the broad expanse of mountains and valley, watching the patterns change as the view became gradually engulfed in sunlight. It was a clear, cold January day. She looked around for her companion, but Happy was nowhere in sight. Wyn strained to listen for any indication of her presence beyond the view from the ledge. She evaluated each sound in anticipation of a meal. A sense of uneasiness spread over her as she confronted the fact that Happy had not returned. Morning melted into noon. Still, Happy did not come. Wyn was alone.

Except for the times when it had been her turn to be the house dog. Wyn had never been alone. There was always at least one other Newfoundland with her in the kennel or free in the big yard. Wyn waited patiently, as

79

only an animal can be patient. Soon, Happy would come trotting around the side of the ledge and greet her. Happy would bring food, and Wyn was hungry, but still her companion did not come. Wyn's anxieties grew. Her loneliness intensified. After nearly two years of constant time together, Happy was not a part of her morning. Through the bonding time of puppyhood and the recent weeks of dependency, Happy had never been far away. But now, she was gone.

A twinge of panic drove Wyn to struggle to her feet. Her shoulder was still extremely painful when she moved, especially getting up or down. But now, the pain in her shoulder seemed secondary to the turmoil tumbling within her. It drove her to move away from the ledge and out on to the trail that led from their hillside home. Wyn hobbled forty feet or so from the security of the ledge. Her distress grew as she looked around for her friend. Her heart pounded. She was experiencing a feeling she had never felt before—real loneliness.

Wyn lowered her head and sniffed the trail but found only faint indications of her companion's scent. Her inner self rebelled at the efforts to go further. So she stood quietly for a while, looking out into the forest. And then she released a single howling complaint, a composite of her misery. The plaintive voice lifted above the pines and drifted down the mountainside to the valley below. The forest creatures heard, but did not respond. The sound faded away into silence. Wyn stood for a time, listening. She felt momentarily better, having rid herself of much of her uneasy feelings. Whining softly, she

LIVE · FOREVER

turned and limped her way back to her refuge to do the only ting she knew to do. She would wait for Happy's return.

Some distance away, Wyn's companion was totally unaware of her plea. The sun was hot on her back, prompting her to move into the shade of a large evergreen. Intently, she watched Will putter away on the hand pump. At daybreak, the two of them had shared a warm breakfast of delicious fried meat, gravy and biscuits. Happy had followed Will across the open yard, drooling at the aroma of her pan of breakfast he held in his hand. She listened to his kind voice talking to her. She waited patiently for him to put the pan on the ground, then wagged her tail gratefully and proceeded to lick up every crumb. The pan looked as clean as if Will had scrubbed it in soapy water. It felt good to share food and companionship with a human. Biscuits, meat and gravy were delicious fare compared to the rabbits and squirrels that had become a major portion of her diet.

During his usual early morning smoke on the porch, Will studied Happy carefully. At daybreak, he had hopped out of bed in a moment of anxiety, hurrying to the door in his nightshirt to see if the big, black dog had stayed with him through the night. And there she was, asleep in the same spot where he'd left her. Only the creaking hinges of the big slab door disturbed her long night's rest on Will's porch. It pleased him to see her waken, look up and wag her tail when she saw him. It was good, he thought, to have company. It was nice to have someone to talk to, a gentle, undemanding companion. She was so quiet . . . such a pleasant dog!

At noon, Will stopped for a meal and coffee. For the past hour, he'd been aware that Happy was restless. He had a gathering feeling that something was bothering her. He stopped work as much to spend time with her as to eat. Willingly, she joined him, sitting for a while with her big head in his lap, absorbing the pleasure of human contact.

It was nice, Will thought, how she would let him work and never get in the way. But if he stopped to rest, then she seemed to feel that it was her turn. She obviously had been with someone who cared about her and gave her time and attention. He wondered again where she came from, what kind of a dog she was, and how she happened to find him on the mountain top. Lost in his thoughts about her, he stopped stroking her until a powerful nudge from her great muzzle jolted him. Will smiled down at the big dog, resumed his attention, and spoke warmly to his companion.

The winter sun's warm rays beat down on Will's back, a reminder that spring would soon arrive. So he spent the afternoon getting his garden plot ready. Many plants were suitable for early planting, while the ground was still cool and moist. As he worked, Will was sensitive to Happy's growing restlessness. It was not his imagination. Her behavior had changed visibly. She paced around the area where he worked, then walked out into the yard, over toward the chicken house and back to him. Gradually, she developed a pattern of travel. On each round, she stopped at the trail leading out of the clearing and into the forest. Once in a while, she drank from the cool water he'd set out for her, then paced her pattern again. Occasionally, she relaxed in the shade for ten minutes or so and watched him work.

Her activity worried Will. He thought for a moment of tying her up so she couldn't leave. He had a good piece of rope in the storage shed. But then he thought of the rough, heavy rope on the luxuriant coat around her neck and dismissed the idea from his mind. Still, he knew now that there were emotions stirring within her. He didn't want to acknowledge the possibility, but the thought kept stealing back into his mind that she was going to leave.

Will wondered if she was merely passing through. Was she on her way to some distant place? He had read of dogs that traveled great distances to get back to their families. He was sure she had a family. "She must be missing them," he thought, "and she is not going to be content to stay here with me." Will got up from his garden patch and walked over to the big animal. For a long time he stood looking down at her lying there in the shade. Her black coat engulfed her huge frame; her beautiful head was lifted in his direction. It made him feel good just to look at her, she was so pretty.

As though she could sense Will's feelings, Happy looked up at him with a curious gaze. Her dark eyes were full of trust. It was not like him to stop his work and come to her. She watched patiently to see what he was going to do. At last, he spoke to her.

"Pretty lady," he said in his deep and gentle voice, "If you must go, I will understand. But I wish . . . " Then he paused for a moment, waiting for the ache in his throat to subside, and his voice trailed away into a whisper, "I wish you could stay here with me."

Will kneeled down by the dog, took her big head between his hands and felt her warmth. She stretched forward with her muzzle and examined his whole face with her nose. This was the closest she had been to the bearded face with the kind voice. She sniffed his eyes, his hair, his beard, then sneezed lightly as if the beard tickled her nose. Reaching out once again to him, she gave him one quick lick up the side of his face.

Will stood. With the Newfoundland kiss coolly evaporating on his cheek, he turned and went back to work in his garden. He knew in his heart that they were friends. He knew also that the dog needed or wanted something that she hadn't found here on the mountain with him. He knew that someday, maybe today, maybe tomorrow, he would look up and the big dog would be gone.

INVISIBLE CONNECTORS

Happy was awake before daylight. She moved from one spot to another on the porch in an effort to quiet the unrest within her. She paced across the porch, jumped off and patrolled the yard, then hopped back onto the porch again and curled up tightly by Will's door, as if that would shut out the uneasy feeling. Still, it would not go away. She stood up, stretched, and shook her body to chase away the last remnants of sleep. But even that did not rid her of the gnawing feeling. At last, it crystallized in her mind. She needed to go to Wyn.

The accidental encounter with Will had met a basic need for Happy . . . human companionship. But however satisfying these moments had been to her, the bonding threads of puppyhood were stronger. Invisible connectors tugged at her as surely as anchor lines. Since the shooting, Happy had assumed a responsibility she

89

could not deny. So now, nudged by her feelings for Wyn, she was driven to leave the comforts of her new friendship. Stopping only long enough for a few laps of water from the bowl at the pump, Happy set off in the early daylight to find Wyn.

She moved easily through the forest, occasionally picking her way through heavy underbrush as she made her way back toward the ledge home to Wyn. For the first time in her life, neither the sight nor smell of small game penetrated her concentration; she was intent on returning to her friend. The closer she got to their quarters, the faster her pace became. Finally, she broke into a gallop, an easy rocking gait that carried her gracefully over the last rise that separated her from her destination. Panting heavily, she bounded around the corner of the ledge and then came to a sliding stop directly over her friend.

Wyn whined in delight at Happy's surprise appearance. Rising almost effortlessly, she stood on her three strong legs to balance herself against Happy's greeting. Wyn felt her loneliness draining away. Happy ran her muzzle over Wyn's entire length, then returned once again to investigate the wounded shoulder. Fluids still seeped from the healing wound. She felt compelled to wash it lightly, as she had done ever since the shooting. When she was satisfied that Wyn was safe, Happy retreated to the inner reaches of the ledge. All her feelings of anxiety were gone now. She lay down on the dirt floor, rested her head between her big paws and slept.

For the moment, Wyn forgot her hunger. She lay down close to Happy. Both dogs drowsed until the rays of the sun crept into their shelter. The warmth spread over them. Happy sat up. For a long time she showed no interest in her surroundings. She shifted from one hip to the other, still sitting, still totally unresponsive to the world around her, not even to Wyn or the soft call of quail in the evening light. Finally, she stood and slowly wandered a short way from the ledge. A Stellar jay shrieked at her sudden presence in his territory.

Happy was full of mixed feelings. She thought of Will, remembering sensations of his hands on her. Yet here she was at the ledge with Wyn, where she wanted to be. Again, thoughts of Will drifted into her consciousness. She wanted to be with him, to hear his voice, and to taste the wonderful biscuits he fed her. These thoughts tapped continually at the serenity of her surroundings, beckoning to her. Much like the jay, who flitted from branch to branch, squawking his warnings, she could not relax. She walked slowly back up the slope, stopped when she reached Wyn and stood looking down at her friend.

Wyn was awake. She knew before she opened her eyes that Happy was standing over her. She stretched, then methodically lifted herself to a standing position, face to face with her black-eyed friend. With each attempt, it was becoming easier for her to move. Wyn watched as Happy turned away and disappeared around the ledge.

It was late afternoon, a good time to be hunting, and Wyn was hungry. As she grew stronger and more active, she had begun to need more food than Happy provided. Wyn watched her friend's actions. Convinced by her own hunger, she interpreted them as an invitation to hunt. She was slowed by her wound, but Wyn willingly followed her woolly friend beyond the security of their quarters and farther away from the ledge than she had been since they first came here.

Wyn enjoyed accompanying Happy on the trail. After more than two weeks of healing and rest, her body was ready for new challenges. Although she still felt discomfort in her shoulder and was still unable to share in the teamwork of hunting, this first journey was a satisfying step toward complete recovery. Wyn watched intently when Happy veered from the path and disappeared into high shrubs. She waited on the trail, standing quietly and listening with great curiosity to the activity as sticks snapped and brush rustled. Then all sounds stopped. Wyn sat down in the gathering dusk and waited. Her ears were alert.

In a few moments, Happy came proudly out of the brush with a ground squirrel swinging from her muzzle. She dropped it in front of Wyn. The hungry dog stretched forward and pulled the furry carcass to her. The tip of her tail wagged as she accepted Happy's wonderful gift. Nudging the squirrel with her nose, Wyn sniffed it once more, drooling now in preparation for the feast. Small though it was, it would provide much needed nourishment.

Happy watched the squirrel disappear. She loved to chase and hunt, but at the moment, she wasn't the least bit interested in eating her prize. During her short time with Will, she had developed a taste for cooked meat, biscuits and gravy. As she watched Wyn devour the squirrel, Happy was thinking of a very different dinner,

COULTER PINE

served in a pan by friendly hands. As Wyn finished her meal, Happy urged her to move on, but she refused, content instead to lie there on the soft earth until dark. Wyn's tongue licked her jaws to remove every bit of squirrel flavor left there. Then she carefully washed her front legs and paws. At last, she felt that she was clean. There was no way now to detect a meal had been eaten except for a few tufts of fur on the ground, which Wyn investigated with her nose and then ignored.

Wyn was content with her first hunt. Although she played a minor part in the event, it was satisfying to to share in the hunting experienced again. When she was ready she stood and turned toward her ledge home. She felt a confidence she had not experienced since the shooting. Wyn had hobbled only a few steps when she became aware of Happy's big body coming toward her in the darkness. She moved over to give her companion space on the trail leading back to the ledge. But Wyn felt Happy lean into her, pressuring her to change direction. Wyn slowed, but her quiet need to return to the ledge caused her to nudge Happy over slightly and move on. Happy woofed a soft warning, then moved ahead of Wyn and stopped. Wyn was surprised to find Happy was blocking her way. Yet, still intent on returning to the safety of her ledge home, she ignored Happy's signal and tried to maneuver past her.

Happy could not communicate to Wyn the wonderful things in store for her at Will's: the kind human . . . his gentle ways . . . the biscuits. Yet inspired by these memories, she tried again to move Wyn in the direction of the cabin. Not understanding, Wyn sat, watched and listened as her companion walked ahead, then returned to sniff at her, then walked away again, away from the ledge. Finally, Happy traveled quite far ahead on the trail. From the black woodland where she disappeared, Wyn heard a single "Woof." It made her stand up and listen.

Happy made no more sounds, but she waited patiently. At last she could hear Wyn coming in her direction, thumping along on three legs. Happy waited for Wyn to reach her. Muzzles met in the darkness, then Happy turned and continued on again with Wyn by her side. Sensing a purpose to Happy's activities, Wyn finally bent to the her friend's persistence and hobbled after her complacently.

They traveled for a while, until the stress on Wyn's body demanded that she rest. Panting quietly, she lay down on the trail and refused to move. There was nothing Happy could do to get her on her feet again. So Happy, too, lay down and waited for Wyn to regain her strength.

Happy woke just at daylight. She stood and stretched, then shook heavily. Her hungry stomach gurgled, and she felt restless. But there would be no biscuits this morning. A noisy raven crossed the sky above her in search of his morning meal. The big bird seemed to remind her that she, too, could hunt for her breakfast. With a parting glance in Wyn's direction, Happy loped off into the woods, heading toward a thicket where she found food enough to silence her hunger. She devoured it on the spot.

When Happy returned, Wyn was up and walking

about on the trail. She, also had sensed the presence of wildlife, but was not yet up to a chase. She looked in Happy's direction expectantly as she heard her approach and walked toward her with anticipation. Happy greeted her eagerly, standing still while Wyn investigated the aroma of breakfast that still clung to her muzzle. That was the only hint of food Happy had for her this morning. There were priorities in Happy's mind that Wyn could not understand, but must accept. Happy again turned onto the trail toward Will's home. Looking back at her companion, she barked a playful, yet demanding invitation to follow.

As the two made their way through the mountain country, Wyn felt better than she had since the shooting. Early in their journey, she stood and tried ever so carefully to put a little weight on her sore leg. But it hurt, and she immediately lifted it again. As the morning wore on, she tried her wounded leg time and again. It was still too sensitive to walk on, but gradually, she found she could put a bit of weight on it when she stood still to rest. Although the terrible soreness remained, she could once again stand on four legs.

Late in the morning, Happy found food for both of them. The meal provided a good chance for Wyn to rest a while. But the inevitable time came when Happy was ready to move on. Persistent, she stood in the trail looking at Wyn, then, as before, she moved on down the trail, looked back and barked her command. Again, Wyn responded.

As she followed behind her companion, Wyn felt her energy renewed by the exercise and her morning meal.

A familiar feeling of courage surged back into her body. She still followed Happy, but old, satisfying feelings of leadership began to surface again. Wyn lifted her head a little higher with a hint of strength and pride. Momentarily forgetting her injury, she made a move in response to her inner feelings of well-being, an attempt to take the lead on the trail. But a new surge of pain reminded her that she was not quite ready to assume the leadership role. Instead, she merely caught up with Happy, greeted her with a muffled sound and an exuberant tail wag, then relaxed again to a hobbling follower's pace . . . at least for the time being.

Wyn didn't feel tired, yet suddenly she realized Happy had was moving faster. She was having trouble keeping up. The great effort was taxing her strength. Looking ahead, Wyn saw her friend break into a gallop and disappear, without ever looking back. Wyn tried her best, but she could not match her companion's speed. Still, her determination carried her along the trail after Happy's scent. It was all she needed to urge her on.

Happy broke out of the forest and into the clearing above the cabin, then stopped abruptly. A quick glance told her all was the same. She could hear the chickens chortling their bedtime serenade. She could see the tool shed, the garden patch, and the old water pump with her dish still below the spout. And there was Will! He was sitting on the porch with his back to her.

Happy rushed to him. With a throaty whine, she thrust her head into his lap, felt his arms around her, and heard his gentle voice as he welcomed her back into his life. Will buried his face in Happy's thick coat. He could hardly believe what was happening. She had really come back! It never occurred to him that she might return. He believed when she disappeared that she needed to be somewhere else and that his cabin had been just a stopping off place along the way on a journey she could not tell him about.

In the long years since May's death, Will had learned to live alone. He had built a good life that left no room for loneliness. Now, sitting on the porch step with the big dog nudging him for attention, he felt his heart reaching out to her with affection. In response, she leaned heavily against him, the weight of her body pressing him hard against the sharp edge of the porch post. He felt helpless, but joyful as she washed his ear and neck and face in her own happiness. "She's been lonely, too," Will thought, as he struggled to regain control of the situation. "She is as glad to see me as I am to have her back again."

Happy eventually calmed and lay down beside him, content as he gently stroked her neck and side. In those moments, Will finally admitted to himself thoughts he had not even let form in his mind until now.

"I have been very lonely without you, dog," he said looking down at Happy. "I haven't been lonely like that for many, many years, not since I lost another lovely lady."

Loving brought many feelings, Will thought. When love was lost there was awful pain, but the joy of companionship, the happiness of being together, the warm memories shared, far surpassed the pain of lost love. Will's fingers burrowed deep into Happy's black coat.

"Welcome back, pretty lady," he said. "Welcome home!"

Wyn trailed her friend to the top of the slope. In the dusk of evening she caught the scent of the man. It stopped her from following Happy down to the clearing, but from her vantage point she could see her friend and the man together on the porch. She watched intently. Her body quivered with both fear and longing.

Will sat on the porch with Happy for nearly two hours. It was a time of healing for both of them, a time needed to heal a loneliness that both Will and Happy felt. Happy dozed, content to be back by Will's side. Occasionally she woke, lifted her head, wagged her tail, then relaxed again. Will knew what she was experiencing. It was the same for him. She'd come back! Out of nowhere the big, black dog had returned to him. He wasn't alone anymore. She was a part of his life once again.

After a time, Will grew drowsy. Happy's deep, rhythmic breathing told him she was sound asleep. He stood and looked up into the starry night, aware of the blackness of the forest that surrounded him. "Where has she been?" He wondered. "And where did she come from?" He leaned down and stroked her once more. He was go glad to have her back. Will reached for the latch on the cabin door and stepped into the glow of a single lighted lamp. The hinges creaked as the door shut between him and the dog. He was sure that when morning came he would find his friendly giant waiting with her usual exuberant greeting. As sleep came to him he was thinking of making breakfast for two.

★ ★ ★ ★ ★

In the forest, Wyn lay curled under the protective cover of a big bush. The day had been a long one, and she needed the rest. Protected by the undergrowth and knowing that Happy was nearby, Wyn slept peacefully until the creaking hinge of Will's cabin door awakened her the next morning.

There was an extra lilt to Will's whistle as he rolled out the soft biscuit dough. He knew, by feel, it was just thick enough to make perfect biscuits, and this morning he took special care to make sure they were perfect. The wood stove was all ready. He knew just how many sticks of kindling it took to make the oven hot enough.

Will had opened the cabin door full of confidence that the dog would still be there waiting for him. She was up in an instant, greeting him with low, throaty sounds, her bushy tail swinging widely from side to side. Now she was waiting patiently for the breakfast of meat, gravy and biscuits that she knew Will had for her.

Usually Will ate before he fed the dog, but this morning he fixed her breakfast first. He carried it out the door to the water pump, talking to her as they walked across the yard. Just then a movement at the edge of the clearing caught Will's eye. He looked up, searching for what he expected to be a coyote.

Instead, he saw a black form standing motionless, partially obscured by the brush. To get a better view, Will moved a few steps forward. In response, the black form backed up, moving behind the bushes to a more protected position. Only a head peered out. Suddenly Will realized what he was looking at. There, before him stood another black dog!

Happy was so intent on the breakfast pan Will was holding, she was not even aware of Wyn's presence. Drooling in anticipation, she woofed a soft reminder at Will. Almost automatically, he put the pan down and then moved slowly toward the other dog at the edge of the clearing. It had to be a companion to his woolly friend, he reasoned. They were almost the same size. His inner sense told him to be cautious. The dog didn't move. It just stood there looking at him.

Will spoke. His voice was reassuring and coaxing. Ever so slowly, he continued to move toward the animal, traveling in a circular path to gain a better view. He could see now that this dog wasn't as big as his friend. It was thin, and its coat wasn't bushy. And it seemed wary. Will stopped and studied the new dog for a long time. Sensing its uneasiness, he backed away a short distance. Still, it just stood there looking at him, and he could sense its fear.

Noticing how thin this dog was, Will turned back to the cabin to get some food. Happy was busy licking her pan clean. In the kitchen, Will hesitated for a moment over his own breakfast, so delightfully hot and fragrant. It made his mouth water. Then he tore off a single biscuit and set it aside. The rest of his meal he scraped into another pan for the new arrival. Then, Will headed back across the clearing and back up the slope.

Wyn watched the man approach. Still she did not move. The man came closer. As Wyn watched him, his image suddenly changed to that of a man on horseback.

Quickly, though, that image was gone, and Wyn could hear a gentle voice speaking to her. The man was still some distance away when the image of the rancher on horseback flashed before her again. Wyn felt panic. Her painful experience had taught her not to trust men. She trembled. Like the other, this human kept coming closer and closer. At the moment he reached the same distance as the rancher had been when he fired, Wyn could see only the rancher. Reliving that awful moment, she whirled and fled into the forest. Wyn cried out in pain and fear as her wounded muscles stretched and tore.

Alerted by the sound of her friend's cry, Happy galloped into the forest after Wyn. It didn't take long to find her. She hadn't gone far. She was lying down under a bush, and her body was shaking violently. Happy sniffed a glad greeting, expecting a response. But none came. Then Happy sniffed at the shoulder wound. It was seeping a little blood. Wanting to stay with Wyn, Happy lay down close by. The injured dog took much comfort in her big companion's presence, and she began to calm.

Will climbed the slope and looked out into the forest. Not far away he could see both dogs. He watched them for a long time, thinking about what had taken place and working out in his mind the line of events that might have led them to his cabin. As the second dog had limped away, he could clearly see the injury to its shoulder. It was a nasty wound. He still could not figure why Happy had come to his cabin the first time, but he now understood why she had become restless and why she had eventually disappeared. It was clear; she had gone to get her friend. Either she had traveled a great distance, or the wounded dog had slowed her journey and kept her away so long.

Will's curiosity about the pair of big black dogs grew as he watched them together in the distance. Surely if they were lost, someone would have posted a notice at the store. But he'd heard no talk of lost dogs when he went down to buy supplies. They had not grown up in the wild, that he was sure of. And they were the same kind of dog. He wondered again about that. What kind of dogs were they? Did they have names?

Will continued watching the pair from a discrete distance. He saw his friend get up occasionally and move to her companion, waving her tail gently in a pleasant greeting before lying down again near the injured dog. Will wondered if it was her pup. But no, the second dog seemed older than his companion. He wondered if it might be a male, and her mate. Yes, that was possible. It was obvious from all he'd observed that they were very close.

At last, Will turned to the duties of his day. Already, the morning was half over. As he worked, he was acutely aware that just over the rise, his friend and companion was offering comfort to another that needed her. It satisfied him just to know she was out there. She had come home to him. She had gone to find her companion and then she'd come home! He was content now to wait for her again. Will knew that when the time was right, she would bring her friend to the cabin.

COYOTE CALL

The young chicken thief lay basking in the warmth of the February sun, feeling the cool ground beneath him, still damp from the night's rain. It was mid-morning. The storm clouds had broken up, and sunlight lifted moisture from the steaming ground into the cool, winter air. The coyote stretched full length, arched his back and relaxed again, content in his wild comfort.

The attack came suddenly, out of nowhere. He was grabbed viciously, shaken, and then released. A firm reminder from the senior male of his pack, the attack was over as fast as it had begun. Soon it would be the mating season, and youngsters were not to take part in the spring ritual. The young coyote stood and shook, then looked around, bewildered and jumpy. This incident marked the third time recently that the alpha male had attacked him.

The pugnacious male stood nearby, next to a female.

Other members of the pack were scattered about the area, two in view and three more out of sight. He could sense their presence even though he could not see them. Not one of the pack seemed the least concerned over the episode. After a few moments, even the young male himself appeared to take it in stride. The big coyote was just reaffirming his place as ranking male. Yet, this third attack stirred unfamiliar feelings in the youngster. He shook again, assembled his dignity, then turned and trotted effortlessly away from the group.

Happy and Wyn had already enjoyed their usual morning romp in the clearing, followed by a generous breakfast. Now, they were basking in the same morning sun that warmed the coyote. The two dogs had been with Will for three weeks. They expected him to come outside at any moment and work as he usually did in the mornings. But Will was busy inside the cabin. The clearing seemed especially quiet without his cheery whistling.

The young coyote had not been near the clearing since his last encounter with Will's giant rooster. Vividly, he remembered the chase through the forest, the gunshot whizzing past him, and the loss of his prize. He had great respect for humans. They were dangerous. But now curiosity, restlessness, and a total lack of anything else to do led him back to the clearing despite his caution.

The coyote's large ears first appeared over the top of the rise behind the chicken house, straining to hear sounds from all directions. Next, his chiseled, narrow muzzle appeared in view, followed by yellow eyes that looked down over the clearing. He could see the hens in their securely fenced enclosure. Then the inquisitive, young male stiffened and cringed as if about to retreat, but his feet did not move. He was completely immobilized. Two black bodies were stretched out in the clearing. His nose told him they were dogs, something new and different on the mountain.

The coyote forgot his plans for another chicken dinner. Instead, with extreme caution, he began an intensive survey of the area surrounding the cabin, looking for clues to the behavior patterns of the two newcomers. Trotting along quickly, he investigated the forest perimeter that surrounded Will's home. He found the place where the dogs entered and left the clearing. He knew they hunted because of the bones and fur and occasional entrails he discovered. Finally, he came upon areas in the forest where the dogs had emptied themselves. There, he sniffed carefully. The coyote's body tingled in an unfamiliar way as he studied the signatures left by the Newfoundlands. As a young male canine, he was responding to the scent of females. It mattered not to him that they were dogs rather than coyotes. He carefully examined the areas again, experiencing new sensations within himself. After a while, he felt compelled to leave his own mark with the strange and stimulating scents. Then, he continued to explore, marking occasionally. His evaluation complete, he drifted silently to the top of the slope again and peered back down into the clearing. He felt satisfied now with his knowledge of the newcomers on the mountain. Without further investigation, he turned and trotted away.

★ ★ ★ ★ ★

Wyn flinched as the door squeaked open. She knew that it would be Will. She had learned that he would not harm her, but she still had moments of fright. For some reason the door hinge alerted her fearful mind that man was coming. Happy, too, heard the squeaking door. She was on her feet and waiting to greet Will.

Wyn stood and wagged her tail when Will spoke to her, but did not approach him. They had a mutual agreement. They were friends from a distance. Wyn gratefully accepted the food prepared for her each day. She longed to join in when Will stroked and patted Happy, yet the fear in her heart was so great that she could not let herself go to him. Will understood and never made an attempt to touch her.

So many times since she had come, Will wished that he could tend her injured shoulder. Stored in his medicine cabinet were many self-care remedies. He had learned their proper use from his parents, who cared for the family's medical needs. He knew, for example, that soothing calendula ointment would help to heal the wound, and arnica lotion would relieve the soreness, but he accepted the fact that he would never have a chance to give the big, black dog that kind of attention.

Wyn could walk on the injured leg now, but she still limped. Will was satisfied as he looked at her. She was healthy and improving rapidly. Her ribby sides had filled in since her arrival in the clearing, and the area of exposed bone was almost completely healed over.

110

BOULDERS

OF HERITAGE AND HEART

Will had little trouble with the idea of having two dogs around. He thoroughly enjoyed Happy's companionship, and if the only way she would stay was to have her friend, then that's the way it would be.

Will knew now that the second dog was also a female and not Happy's mate as he'd first guessed. He'd noticed that the pair would disappear into the forest and return exhausted, but not hungry. So he figured they were good hunters. Their company was pleasant to him, and he had not seen a coyote near the place since their arrival, making him especially grateful for their presence.

The days blended into weeks, and late winter gave way to spring. The spring sun warmed the vegetation that surrounded the little mountain retreat. New life swelled the tiny bud caps on branches. Soon, the caps would fall away and the growth of another year would burst forth from stems and mushroom into the thousands of shapes and shades of spring green.

Will's garden was up in little rows that doubled in size daily. The spring rains and warm sun were working their magic. The promise of radishes and lettuce and sweet, crispy onions fresh from his garden motivated Will as he tended the little patch, watching his treasures grow into bite-sized portions.

Life settled into a pleasant pattern of contentment for the trio at the cabin. Each found a special set of daily duties that gave meaning and purpose to living. Wyn was the self-appointed overseer. Totally in keeping with her dominant role in the world, she established her resting place at the top of the clearing, overlooking the homestead. From that vantage point, she could see all the buildings, the garden, the steps to the porch, and the water pump. Her overlook was not far from the chicken house and the trail that led into the forest.

Most of the time, Wyn's attention was directed toward the cabin area where Will was often active. Occasionally, however, she amused herself by watching the mindless activities of the hens, but their constant scratching, pecking, and feather ruffling could not hold her attention for long. Will's new young rooster was beginning to show comb and wattles, finally making him distinguishable from the silly hens. He showed no more intelligence, however.

Wyn's inventive mind developed a game she played against the hens whenever she was on sentry duty near the chicken house. She set up an imaginary line inside one corner of the fenced enclosure, and if a particularly annoying bird crossed that line, the big dog charged the fence and sent the chicken fluttering and squawking back to the protection of the flock.

Since Wyn never touched the fence in her mock attacks and no harm came to his foolish birds, Will, with a feeling of kindred spirit, accepted chicken harassment as an allowable amusement for her. Besides, he knew he had no worries about coyotes as long as she dog kept her vigil at the top of the slope. This spring had been an easy time, thanks to her.

★ ★ ★ ★ ★

Spring had its influence on Wyn as it did on the budding forest around her. Will noticed her growing restlessness. She paced about the clearing and often disappeared for a short hunt alone. A few times during the past week, she had challenged Happy to little mock duels, thrusting her muzzle and neck firmly over Happy's shoulders and forcing her body into her larger companion.

Happy's only response was to stand benignly, enduring a challenge or two. If the aggressor pushed for more, Happy simply rolled over on her back, woolly belly up and all four feet pawing the air. This way she gave notice that she had no intentions of responding aggressively to the challenge. And so it was that Happy kept the peace. Will watched her and understood. He was grateful for her peacemaking.

One sunny afternoon, Wyn got up from a nap in her favorite spot and stretched lazily. Her healing shoulder allowed her to move more freely now. She could lower her chest nearly all the way to the ground in a good stretch. She strolled off to the upper edge of the clearing and stood looking out into a forest that was dressed in lacy spring green.

A quick movement caught her eye, a grey-brown form in the distance. In reaction to her appearance at the top of the hill, the form vanished. Wyn ran at full speed directly toward the spot where she had seen the animal. It felt good to stretch and run. She felt strong as she powered her body over the trail. She was aware of her shoulder, but there was no pain now, just soreness. Wyn knew the mountain well. She stopped at precisely the spot where the animal had been. There was no need to chase it; experience told her it was gone. Instead, she concentrated on the strong scent the animal had left behind. Her upper lips drooped toward the dirt as her nostrils went over and over the coyote's signature. She snuffled and sneezed, then sniffed some more. This was the same urine scent that she found frequently near the chicken house. She turned her body to leave her mark in precisely the same area where the coyote had left his. The messages had been exchanged.

Wyn stood and looked in the direction of the coyote's departure. She knew it was a male, but she did not feel threatened by his presence in her territory. Curious, she trotted off along his trail. She traveled a few hundred yards after the elusive scent, then lost interest. Again she left her mark, then turned and ambled in a half circle around the edge of her forest home, sniffing and leaving scent in various places along the way.

The young coyote had returned to the clearing many times, his original intent was to snatch another of Will's tasty hens. But the presence of the two big dogs deterred him, as Will hoped it would. The hen population remained intact and relatively undisturbed. Instead, the dogs became the focal point of the coyote's curiosity. With the coyotes' mating season in full swing, the young females were pleasingly fragrant to the young male.

He was nearly two, whelped on the mountain at almost the same time Wyn had been whelped in the west. For his age, he was an exceptional specimen; large, strong and powerful, thus prompting antagonism from the alpha male. But for all of his threats and dominant male behavior, the senior coyote could not quiet the adult drives that were stirring within this maturing young coyote. He was not yet ready to do battle among his own, but he was repeatedly drawn to the woods trail that led toward the clearing and the scent of other females.

Countless journeys took him near the clearing. For weeks, he had been coming back again and again to seek out the newcomers on the mountain. He knew their patterns of behavior. He knew where they hunted. He often trailed behind them at a safe distance and watched their clumsy, but successful, attempts to seek food. These two big animals intrigued him. He was so preoccupied with his activities that he often returned to the coyote family group exhausted and hardly responsive. At least his withdrawal from the group prevented more encounters with the ranking male.

Once, however, he got a bit careless and allowed himself to follow too closely to the hunting Newfoundlands. Wyn spotted him in open country and broke into a full run with Happy close behind her. Together, the two dogs chased the coyote into the rugged hillside where his agility allowed him to escape. This was the closest encounter so far. It gave Wyn the opportunity to put sight and scent together. She now knew what it was that had that particular odor. She knew this was the same animal that often came close to the cabin and left his distinctive mark, the same animal she had chased behind the chicken house, the one that always influenced her to leave her mark where he left his. Their signatures had been exchanged many times in the forest. But only twice had Wyn actually seen him, once in the forest behind Will's cabin and again this time in the open country.

It was late afternoon. Wyn and Happy returned to the cabin and drank from the big pan at the pump. Each in turn splashed and pawed in the cold water. By now, Will was used to this ritual. He calmly rinsed and refilled the pan until their appetite for water play was satisfied. Then he watched as each dog retired to her favorite resting spot.

The encounter with the coyote had given Wyn the exercise she needed. She loved a good chase. A moving target was compelling. She liked to come home afterwards and sprawl happily on the crest of the slope, surveying the peaceful scene below. The pan of water under the pump looked inviting.

Wyn moved down the hill for another drink. She had learned to expect certain comforts from her life here, such as the clean water and the good meals from Will's kitchen. Like her kennel home, this place offered certain assurances—food and water, a kind voice, a place to rest, security.

Wyn drank until she was satisfied, then made her way back to the upper edge of the clearing. Stretching out lazily, she slept in peace as the late afternoon breezes blew gently over her shining black body. The warm March sun filtered down on her through the pines, releasing a marvelous aroma. The familiar scent drifted heavily over the sleeping dog and mingled with her dreams, again stirring Wyn's deep attachment to her human. Just as before when she'd watched the young calf play, there was magic in the pine. As the sweet scent penetrated the sleeping dog's mind, it brought once again the image of a peaceful place with cool green grass and long evergreen shadows. Deep in sleep, Wyn's mind released the vision of the elegant, old brick farm home and the screened porch. Again her body felt anticipation. She was waiting for someone. Then, in her dreams, her human came to her as she had so many times before. She could hear the voice. She could feel the gentle hand on her neck and back. As Wyn's visions whirled, her tail wagged with happiness.

The big dog woke suddenly and sat up, as she brought herself to reality. The shared moments with her human in the dream had left her with lingering feelings that disturbed her. They made her feel restless, plaguing her with a dull sensation of wanting something. The feeling was so strong that it made her get up and walk. She had frequently felt discontent vibrating within her in recent weeks, but this was a different kind of need. She just couldn't free herself from the growing desire stirred up by her dream.

Will came out on the cabin porch and called to both dogs. He held a pan of dinner for each. It was at that moment that Wyn was able to make sense of her feelings. It was human contact that she longed for. She stood for a time and watched Will as he carried her food toward her. In the evening light, Will could see a strange expression in Wyn's eyes. He didn't think it was pain or fear. No, it was definitely not the fear he had seen the day he first met her. Still the sensitive man could see the need in her eyes. But he could not know that her longing was for another human far away.

Will was curious. He watched her as she ate. When she was finished, he walked over and picked up the empty pan. Wyn stood looking at him, wagged her tail from side to side then turned and disappeared into the darkening forest.

Her restless drive took her a great distance from the cabin. She kept moving far into the night. Had she not paused to drink from a tiny stream, she might have kept moving even longer. But the cool water was fresh and sweet. She lapped at it for a long time, rested, then lapped some more. Her body began to relax. The sound of the water was pleasant as it bubbled over the rocky bed and splashed down into little waterfalls. Suddenly, Wyn felt tired. She began to search for a sheltered place to sleep.

It was not her intent to run away from Happy and Will and her life there at the little cabin. She was being pulled away. Wyn had been deeply stirred by her dream. Events of the last three months had repressed her natural desires to return to her home.

Now, in her new restlessness, she wanted her human. The dream experience had been as real to her as if she had actually sat with her human companion. The caresses, the stroking, and the gentle voice were all as indelibly engraved in her memory as a real experience. It was her longing for one human scent and one particular voice that drove her into the forest in search of home.

As she lay near the little stream, listening to its gentle rhythms and liquid serenade, she felt that longing even more. All of the misty visions that would not come to her two months ago had now fully materialized. Deep within her, she felt the need to seek out her human. Overpowered by her loneliness, Wyn lifted her muzzle to the night sky. From her throat drifted a deep, soft, lonely call for her special person.

Wyn was too far away for Will or even Happy to pick up the plaintive sound as it drifted away into the darkness. But she was not alone. Large ears on a chiseled face turned immediately in the direction of her plea. Then the elegant, grey-brown body of the young coyote stiffened, and he, too, lifted his muzzle skyward, speaking back to her in the darkness. He sounded an abrupt avalanche of yapping retorts and then, as if to mimic her style, one long throaty call.

Wyn lifted her head, her ears alert, and listened to the coyote's call. Then, with a sigh, she put her muzzle down between her big front paws and slept.

NATURE'S DICTATE

Wyn stood and shook her body, freeing her coat of sand and a few tiny leaves and twigs. She went to the stream to drink and as she raised her head, she became aware that she was not alone. The familiar scent in her nostrils indicated the coyote was nearby. She looked for him. And there he was, standing above her, on the side of the hill, watching her intently. When she sighted him, he did not move until she made a charge in his direction; then he vanished. Her curiosity led her along his trail for a short distance, but she followed only half heartedly, then turned and ambled back to the stream.

Wyn was lonely for her special human. The restlessness would not be quieted. It was triggered not only by her growing sense of longing, but also by hormonal dictates. It was spring and Wyn would soon be in heat. It was in response to those signals that her coyote companion followed at a discrete distance.

123

Victim to her abounding curiosity and joy of freedom, Wyn had traveled far from her home. Delayed by a gun shot, the ensuing weeks of healing allowed her bond with Happy to grow stronger. But her acquaintance with Will served only to keep alive the thoughts of another human she wanted badly to find.

Wyn's shoulder rarely bothered her anymore. Scar tissue had closed over the wound and sealed out the possibility of infection. Some of the shoulder was so badly damaged that it would never grow a new coat of hair. In other areas around the edges of the wound, the bare skin was already covered with new, shining black hair that left little indication of the terrible incident in the pasture.

For most of the day, Wyn continued north. Her desire to find her way home mingled with lingering feelings of wanting to return to Happy. By now, she was quite accustomed to her coyote attendant. Occasionally, she looked back to him. He was always there, close enough so that she could see the steady gaze of his yellow eyes.

From time to time, she launched a mock attack toward him, but it never seemed to deter him from his desire to trail after her. And so, in a matter of a few days she came to accept his presence. When she looked back and fully expected him to be there.

For three days, the unlikely duo made their way through the mountain country. Wyn was driven to keep moving; the coyote, eager to follow at a safe distance.

One time, Wyn looked back, and the coyote was gone. She stopped and turned, facing back down the trail. Accustomed to his presence, she did not want to

INTERIOR LIVE OAK

go on without him. She sat down, looking and listening for him. After a while he appeared, holding a ground squirrel in his mouth. When he saw her, he stopped, with the squirrel swinging loosely from his jaws. Since she was sitting still, facing him, he walked to within a few yards of her and lay down. With great interest, she watched him make a quick meal of the squirrel.

Wyn studied this creature's ability to appear and disappear with no sound. When she and Happy hunted, she listened to Happy's crashing, lumbering movements in the brush. That was a part of their hunting pattern. Now, with the coyote, she was learning there was another way. He was a swift and silent hunter, and Wyn saw that he was successful.

She was hungry. Saliva ran in a thin stream from her mouth and floated gently on the light breeze. She remembered the pan of biscuits and meat that Will put before her with his steady hand and gentle words. Today, there was no pan of food for her. Like the coyote, she must hunt for her meal. And she must hunt alone.

The warming days wielded their influence on Wyn. Her age and the season made her more and more appealing to the coyote, as her body responded naturally to the patterns of her species. During the next few days, a few drops of blood appeared where she had been sitting. Wyn's estrus had begun. Again, her need to find her human family was suppressed, as she responded to a more urgent need. Wyn was ready to choose a mate.

Wyn's travel slowed considerably. She was finding food and water and was not unhappy in her present circumstance. She accepted the companionship of her coyote friend. During the next few days, she and the coyote established an area within which they traveled and hunted. Wyn's self-appointed mate watched her attentively. Every time she emptied herself, the coyote would examine the area carefully, then cover her scent with his own urine. In his way he announced to any would-be suitors in the area that Wyn was his.

Occasionally she burst into fits of foolish play. Grabbing a stick, she ran around him, shaking her head invitingly, urging him to chase. This was a typical game she had played with Happy or her human, but the coyote seemed at a loss to interpret exactly what his part in this new game should be. Wyn dropped the stick and pounced toward her new friend, stopping stiff-legged in front of him, nudging him in the side with her muzzle and then dashing away. This he understood, and he responded, leaping after her in a wild game of chase. Wyn was by far the larger of the two, taller and much heavier. Occasionally, she pawed the coyote on his shoulder and forced him to the ground. He rolled to his feet, stiffened, and bounded off playfully.

Usually, after an exhausting roughhouse game of tag and wrestle, he responded with a serenade. Sitting in front of her, nearly muzzle to muzzle, the handsome male lifted his voice in a lusty song to the black lady he had chosen for his own. Wyn was frequently so moved by his stirring lyrics that she joined in, mimicking his posture and style. Though her own deep vibrations were no match for his in variety, they seemed to encourage him to improvise even more. The unlikely duet filled the mountains and valleys with its unique eloquence.

The combined voices announced to all creatures of the wild that the pair's bonding was complete. Wyn and her new mate each had to make allowances for the fact that one was wild and one was domestic. Each brought separate behaviors to their union, although many of their instincts were similar. The Newfoundland could equal the coyote in intelligence, and she was quick to learn when his ways were better. She was a constant challenge to him for there were drives and motivations within her that he could sense, but, in his wildness, could not comprehend. During the days of her estrus, wherever she went her suitor was her constant shadow.

The coyote became increasingly curious about Wyn's body. He had even attempted to mount her, an action that caused his usually quiet, pleasant companion to become suddenly transformed into a raging ball of fury. She lashed out at him, jaws snapping, white teeth bared in a firm warning that she would not accept his overtures. Then, coquettishly, she invited him to play, thrusting her hindquarters into his chest, bumping him solidly. Yet each time he attempted to mount her, the game ended in another furious warning.

After a few more days, she developed a more receptive attitude toward her young suitor. As they played, she began swinging her body into him and standing receptively. In the natural progression of their courtship, the time had come for mating. An experienced male could have responded to her willingness deftly. But Wyn's larger size and the coyote's inexperiences presented the young male with a challenge. Yet, during the next five days Wyn and the coyote united in the bonding that would result in their first family.

On the sixth day, a sunny afternoon, the young male came to his sleeping companion and playfully nudged her to wakefulness. Wyn greeted him and joined him in their usual game of chase and mock attack. But when the coyote attempted to mount her, Wyn again turned on him with teeth bared, warning him off. Estrus was over. He stood facing her with his head held high. She came at him again, grabbed him on the shoulder for a menacing shake, then released her hold. Facing him, she curled her lip to show gleaming white fangs. The young male understood her dictate clearly. His pride wilted before her. Whining a soft complaint, he circled and made one last, half-hearted move toward her. She growled loudly at his approach. Bewildered, he turned away, walked a few yards from her and lay down. He watched her for a while, then went to sleep.

In the weeks that followed, the young Newfoundland would benefit greatly from her choice of a wild mate. The domestic dog is a persistent suitor. Males collect in groups to follow a bitch in season. During the breeding, they scuffle and scrap to ensure that the litter is fathered by more than one sire. But, when the female's appeal disappears, so do the male dogs. Meanwhile, the female trots home to await motherhood in the company of her careless human family. She neither expects nor receives any acknowledgement of her litter from the once persistent and attentive sires.

But the dictates of the coyote are vastly different. Wyn's attentive mate remained so. He had chosen the black companion for his own. Now, he stayed with her. She was a part of his new life. His wild ways made him her protector.

TEN

YEARNINGS

Wyn dug furiously at the hard earth. Dirt flew out between her hind legs as her powerful saucer-shaped paws and hard nails penetrated deeper into the squirrel's tunnel. Alternately, she dug, stopped to snuffle in the hole, then dug some more, sneezing occasionally to clear her scent cells. The cavern got larger as the mound of soft earth built up beneath her.

The maze of tunnels had been skillfully built beneath the tough roots of a manzanita bush. They served as an effective barrier against creatures who had tried in vain to excavate the squirrel from his underground refuge. Many times before, the little animal's hideaway had saved his life.

But Wyn's persistence and strength brought danger closer than usual. Gradually, her paws were reaching much farther than any past intruder had been able to penetrate. But the clever little squirrel had one more safety device. A few feet from the root base of his cozy home, he had dug an emergency exit. So, while Wyn continued her frenzied digging at the front door, the ground squirrel simply made his way through the long tunnel toward his escape hatch.

The digging stopped, and the little animal paused and waited. He was completely silent within his safety tunnel. The squirrel flinched when he heard the snuffling noise again. Wyn dug with increased determination as his enticing scent penetrated her sensitive nose and spurred her on.

Sensing the increased energy of his pursuer, the squirrel crouched for just a moment at the back entrance, then hurled himself through his safety exit far from the menacing paws of the determined Newfoundland. In the next instant, a lightening swift action painlessly snapped the life from the little rodent. When he leaped out the back entrance of his burrow, he had literally thrown himself into the jaws of the waiting coyote.

One quick yip from the coyote communicated to Wyn that their mission was a success. Wyn stopped digging immediately and drew herself out from under the manzanita branches. A look of pride and perhaps even a little amusement showed in her eyes. Her head and neck were red from the soil still clinging to her thick coat. Even the black of her nose was coated with red earth. She shook vigorously.

The young male carried his prize a few steps toward Wyn and halted. His head was up, his tail carried high. The pleasure of this successful moment registered in his eyes. In recent weeks, the pair had perfected this

MANZANITA

maneuver. Frequently, it brought them success. Each seemed to gain great pleasure from the team project. The squirrel was a large one. Its weight felt good in the coyote's mouth. He moved toward Wyn and, as he had done many times before, he presented his mate with a gift.

The easy days of spring continued. The air warmed on the mountain. The slopes and open fields burst into bloom. The season's crop of young rabbits grew to a tasty size. Inexperienced, they were easy prey for the two hunters. Wyn and her coyote mate hunted together a great deal of the time. They knew their range well—where other coyotes lived, how to find good-flowing streams, where the best hunting areas were.

During the next few weeks, the pair dug two separate dens. Wyn clearly preferred one to the other. She spent much time in this unfinished shelter, warm with sunny exposure in the mornings, yet shaded during the hot afternoons. Its location gave her a good vantage point to look down over the sprawling valley and a lightly forested area. The trail leading to the den could be approached only from below, which satisfied some sense of needed security within her. Here, she could stand guard, watchful and secure in the place she now called home.

Frequently, Wyn's mate would leave her to go hunting at night. This habit of his was another major difference between them. Although they spent much of the daytime hours together and even hunted together in the early evenings, Wyn rarely accompanied him at night dark. Yet when darkness set in, the coyote became restless. After a while, he would rise silently to his feet and disappear into the night. Often Wyn was asleep and did not know when he left. During the night, coyote voices sometimes stirred her. Though she did not always know what it meant when he exchanged calls with his own kind, she knew which voice was his.

And so, their pattern of living became firmly established. Some of their lives they shared, some they lived separately, depending on the inherent needs of each. All in all, their daily lives blended into a satisfying companionship.

Continuing changes affected Wyn and her mate. Their life at the den could not go on in endless rounds of play, hunting, and resting. Wyn was into the second trimester of gestation. Her body's demands had begun to influence her life, and consequently, his life as well.

Most obviously, Wyn's pregnancy heightened her natural beauty. Thanks to her active everyday life on the mountain, she was in prime physical condition. Under her thickening black coat, her body rippled with firm muscles. It wasn't at all apparent that she had put on weight, but there was a bloom about her that clearly indicated all was well. By contrast, spring had taken its toll on the young coyote's appearance. He was a pathetic sight. His outer winter coat was dry and falling out in clumps. In a matter of a few weeks, however, a glistening new summer coat would show off his handsome young physique.

Wyn's pregnancy also caused changes in her behavior. Even before daylight, a deep hunger brought her to an uneasy wakefulness. Her need for more food grew in intensity day by day. She began taking food aggressively from her mate after a kill. Bending to her will, the coyote gave up his share without rebuke.

But there was another feeling growing within her. It began as a stirring restlessness, a dull feeling of discontent. Even with her hunger stilled by a satisfying meal, she felt a longing that did not cease. As her time in whelp lengthened from four weeks to five, then to nearly six weeks, Wyn's feelings localized into two distinct areas of need: more food and a need for human companionship. Both sensations drove her on long journeys away from the den.

At six weeks in whelp, Wyn returned to the den after a morning hunt and sprawled in her favorite spot, gazing out over the peaceful valley. The coyote was nowhere to be seen. Wyn should have been content, but she wasn't. She shifted restlessly from place to place near the den entrance. Threads of life with Happy and Will began to tighten their hold on her freedom. Once again, the great division between the wild canine and the domestic dog came into play. Had she been able to convert completely to the ways of her wild companion, she would have been content to give birth to her young at the den. It had been a place of security for many weeks now.

But Wyn's emotional ties to Happy and her need for human contact were strong and deep. They beckoned to her. Happy was comfort. So was Will. She was drawn to the place where she had known their comfort. Will would be there with his kind voice and a pan of meat and fragrant gravy. Wyn drooled as she remembered.

138

At last, in response to her internal needs, Wyn rose to her feet, trotted away from the den, and never looked back. She headed directly for the cabin, Happy's companionship and Will's generosity.

Later, when the coyote searched the den area, he knew intuitively that Wyn was gone. He had been aware of her growing restlessness. He'd felt her change of behavior in subtle, instinctive ways. Curious about her disappearance, however, he set off trailing her scent. Although she had been gone for hours, the trail was clear. Head down, nose to the ground, he followed his mate unerringly.

Slightly weary and very hungry, Wyn increased her pace when she caught the first scent of Happy. Her body tingled with anticipation and new energy as she neared her destination. Motivated by her strong drives, she had traveled four hours. Now, Will's scent mingled with Happy's; they drifted sweetly into her nostrils. As she closed the final distance, eagerness and an elated feeling drove her to break into a gallop. She rushed headlong out of the forest and into the clearing, then scuffed to a halt. Pebbles rippled underfoot and little dust clouds settled about her as she stood tall and silent, looking about the friendly surroundings.

The soft noises of Wyn's arrival in the clearing gently nudged Happy from her afternoon slumber. Lifting her head drowsily, she peered out from her shady spot. When she realized there was an intruder on the property, she came fully awake and jumped to her feet. She sounded a loud warning bark for Will and then a low growl, steady and ominous, aimed in the direction of the animal at the distant end of the clearing. It was rare that anything or anyone ever appeared near the cabin, but Happy was always on guard as protector of her territory.

Wyn's attention focused now on the disgruntled Newfoundland coming toward her. She lifted her tail, flagging it gently from side to side, yet stood her ground and waited as her friend came closer and closer. Wyn understood fully what Happy was feeling. Her tail continued its gentle signal, indicating no fear or intention of aggression. By now Will had appeared at the door to the cabin. He had learned long ago never to be surprised at anything where the black dog was concerned. Now, he felt privileged to witness the reunion of these two old friends.

Happy stopped and studied the intruder. She lifted her muzzle and tested the air for scent, but there was no breeze to answer the question. She could sense immediately that the visitor was peaceful, yet it would go against all of her instincts to welcome a strange dog to her territory. Cautiously, she continued to close the gap between them. Wyn still did not move, save for the gently waving tail.

Wyn's watched her companion's step-by-step approach. Happy's head was down and her tail extended. The hair on her back and neck stood up, giving her a larger than life appearance, as she challenged the intruder.

Then, abruptly, she stood straight and tall for a moment, mimicking Wyn's posture. At last, she recognized her returning friend and rushed to greet her. Her whole body wriggled and squirmed in a completely foolish outpouring of joy, and perhaps embarrassment at her brash behavior. Happy sniffed Wyn's muzzle and eyes, then her entire body. Together, the two friends reared up on their hind legs, pawed at each other, then dropped and ran in great circles in the clearing.

Will watched the playful antics of the two dogs with a twinkle in his eyes. "Well, I'll be darned," he said aloud, "I never thought I'd see that animal again!" He watched as the two spent themselves in puppylike romping.

When at last they tired, they turned toward the cabin. With tongues lolling and bodies heaving for breath, the two friends ambled up the slope in search of water. Wyn knew the pan would be there, by the pump, full and fresh and waiting.

Will watched from the porch as Wyn drank first, gulping, and resting, then gulping again. After her, Happy moved to the pan, sniffed over the water then took one small lap, as if tasting it. Then she drank a little more. Wyn drank again when Happy was through, then found a resting place in the late afternoon shade to stretch and relax. The reunion was as satisfying to Will as it was to both dogs.

Wyn looked about the clearing. The cabin, the garden, the chicken house and fenced yard for the fluttery birds . . . all were as she remembered. She saw Will standing on the porch and started toward him, wagging a greeting. He spoke to her gently, "Welcome home, Black Dog." Wyn suddenly felt very tired. She returned to her place in the clearing and dug and scratched at the soil under her belly. Scraping away the surface soil with her paw, she nestled onto the cool earth. With Happy breathing heavily nearby, Wyn stretched full length on her side and relaxed. She reveled in her feelings of contentment. Her journey was over.

Will moved from the porch and walked up the slope to where the dogs lay. He stood looking down at them. Happy lifted her head and gazed at him, wagging her tail. Wearily and without moving her head, Wyn opened her eyes and looked up at Will. She had no fear of him; she had learned long ago that he would not try to touch her. In a trusting gesture, her tail brushed back and forth in the dirt as he stood over her.

Will studied her carefully. She was in good health. Her coat was thick and shining. "She's put on some weight," he thought, "Looks heavy around the middle." He was mildly curious about where she had been, and why she'd chosen to return to them after so long. "They were mighty glad to see one another again," Will mused. It was obvious that the two dogs were very close. Their attachment was deep, deeper than he had ever estimated.

"Well Lady," Will said to Happy, "We have another mouth to feed. And if she's going to be around, we better give her a name."

ENCOUNTERS

Happy dozed contentedly by the cabin door. The night air was crisp and chill, stars glittered in the black sky like jewels sprinkled across the universe. Nearby, Wyn snuggled into a ball to sleep. She felt at peace as she spent her first night back home on the mountain with Happy and Will. Gone was the constant hunger that had plagued her. Gone, too, were her nagging feelings of loneliness. She breathed deeply and fell into a sound sleep. The mercury in the thermometer on Will's porch dropped below freezing. The two dogs' heavy coats insulated them from the cold, and they felt no discomfort.

In the distance, a coyote band tuned up for a yodeling session. They were a part of the pack that Wyn's mate belonged to. A lone coyote voice answered them in the darkness. It stirred her dreamless sleep, but she did not waken.

In the pre-dawn darkness, an animal appeared in the clearing. It moved into the open a few yards, explored carefully, then receded into the safety of the woodlands. Soundlessly, it circled the clearing, appearing again at the top of the slope directly behind where Wyn lay sleeping.

Wyn's keen senses increased her awareness even in sleep. She awoke suddenly and opened her eyes, but did not move. She was acutely aware that another animal was nearby. She had neither heard nor smelled anything, but she knew. She waited for some indication of what was there. Her ears strained in an attempt to catch any sound in the wooded area behind her. Her nostrils tested the air. She was tense.

One soft yap told her everything. He had followed her! As the young coyote came toward her, she stood to greet him, her tail wagging. No reproach or inquiry marked their joyous meeting. Quickly, they headed off into the darkness. Neither was interested in hunting. Rather, they were captivated by curiosity as they explored the hills and valleys they had not seen for many weeks. Once-dry stream beds were now flowing full with spring runoff. Familiar water holes were brimming with clean rainwater.

The sound of little waterfalls splashing into deep pools triggered in Wyn an irresistible urge to wade and drink, run and splash in the cool mountain water. Her patient companion watched. At last, he waded into a pool, stood with all four feet in the shallow water, and lapped up a few swallows, but he showed no desire to join in her aquatic frolic.

146

The air was filled with a mingling of delicate fragrances of blooming shrubs and spring flowers. The coyote seemed especially lighthearted as they moved through remembered haunts. With all of Wyn's anxieties put aside now, she could join him in complete abandon, as together they revisited and explored the mountain near Will's cabin.

Just after daylight the pair returned to the top of the slope overlooking the clearing. With the first stirrings inside the cabin, however, the coyote grew uneasy and restless. He paced off into the forest, then returned to Wyn. Standing over her, he nudged her with his muzzle in an attempt to get her to move, then trotted off again. After only a few paces, he turned and called to her softly. But Wyn did not respond. In her mind, she was home. She understood what he wanted, but her deep desire for Happy's companionship and a good food supply had brought her here. There was no way she could communicate her domestic needs to her wild mate. The awareness of a nearby human finally drove the coyote away. Leaving his mate behind, he loped off alone into the forest.

★ ★ ★ ★ ★

During the weeks that followed, Wyn began each day with Will's tasty food and shared the hours with her friends in the cabin clearing. It was almost as if she had never gone away. Will was constantly aware of the lasting bond between the two dogs. It seemed to him that it grew stronger as the days went by.

Will still wanted to name his Lady's big friend. She

COULTER   PINE CONE

was a strong, powerful dog, yet distant. He had a gut feeling that she could explode in fury if the occasion warranted. Maybe "Storm" or "Stormy?" But no, she wasn't stormy by nature. Actually, she was quite calm. Although different in many ways, she had the same gentle aura about her that his Lady had. He admired this dog. There was a smoldering within her that hinted of innate courage and the ability to survive, even against the odds. She was proud and dignified, and very wise. She carried herself with almost regal bearing. "Perhaps Queen or Royal?" Will tested each name out loud. No. The mental process intrigued Will, and at the same time, frustrated him. How could you give a dog like this a name? In the end, he continued to call her "Black Dog."

Will looked at both animals. "Black Dog" was in peak condition. He marveled at her shining coat. Although it lay closer to her body than the woolly Lady's did, it fluffed and swirled, thick and wavy, glistening with the bloom of good health. By contrast, Lady's coat had developed a brownish hue and was beginning to fall out in little tufts over the rump and shoulders. Will leaned over and plucked out a few of the old brown clumps. Holding them between thumb and fingers, he studied how the tiny hairs twisted together, preparing to slip cleanly away from Lady's body, and he marveled at nature's way of caring for her own.

★ ★ ★ ★ ★

Late one afternoon, Will strolled to the top of the slope, Wyn's food pan in his hand, but she was not there. Looking out across the forest, he saw her coming, and behind her, the quick movements of a startled coyote disappearing into the brush. Suddenly, the whole story became clear to him. She had a coyote for a mate! They must travel together, he thought. That would account for her absences from the cabin without Lady. It would explain the occasional days she slept so soundly late into the morning. She'd been out running at night with that coyote!

"So that's your secret, Black Dog!" Will chuckled as Wyn greeted him. Her tail wagged, and she looked up expectantly at the morning meal she knew was hers. "You've got yourself a coyote companion," he said teasingly. "He probably likes chickens, too." He put the pan down for her. "And I expect that he is responsible for the 'big around the middle' look of you these days." Will studied her with renewed interest as she gulped down her breakfast. "Eat, Black, eat," he said warmly. "If you're going to have little ones soon, then you need a lot of good food."

When Wyn had finished, Will picked up the empty pan and started for the cabin. He remembered how he'd enjoyed playing with little pups as a young boy. It pleased him to think about a litter of puppies running around the cabin. Over breakfast, he told Happy of his discovery. She looked at him curiously. She was not used to a constant stream of patter from this man. She studied him now, trying desperately to understand what he was saying, but knowing only that he was pleased about something.

Weeks before, during Wyn's absence, Will had locked Happy up securely during her season. He'd learned from his dad about the ways of female dogs at times. So, he knew when he saw a few drops of blood on the cabin porch where Happy slept that it was time to confine her if he didn't want pups. Keeping the chickens housed in their coop, he'd given Happy the hen yard. He knew it was secure. It even had a wire top for extra security against the possibility of a dog visiting from somewhere else on the mountain. Three weeks later, Will freed her once more and sighed in relief, knowing he wouldn't have to find homes for pups. Yet today, the thought of pups didn't bother him at all.

After breakfast, as he wiped his cast-iron skillet clean, he wondered if they would be black, solid black and shiny like the pan. Yes, he decided. They would be shiny like their mother. Black and shiny. Their coats would glisten in the sun just like hers. Would the coyote color come through all that black? Will didn't know.

He also didn't know that the coyote and Wyn had other ideas about their family. Running together through the forest surrounding the cabin, they covered the whole territory. One night during their travels, the male found a good place for a den and began to work on the spot that would be home for them and the expected pups. Wyn joined him in the excavation project. The den location was good, and when the opening was large enough Wyn could crawl inside. Yet even after many days of digging and scraping, something never seemed quite right to her. She wasn't exactly dissatisfied with her new home, but her natural urges drove her to paw away at it time and time again. Occasionally, she lay down in the shelter of the little cavern after a digging spree, but she never stayed for long. By instinct, she preferred to be outside the den where she was able to see all around her.

The coyote rested easier each time he returned to the site and found his mate snoozing quietly. There came a time each day, however, when he was faced once again with the frustration of having a domestic mate. When Wyn felt the need for her other companions, she would suddenly get to her feet and be on her way back to her other world.

For the moment, Wyn's life was complete. All of her needs were fulfilled. She had food, water, the comfort of old friends, and the challenge of a faithful, wild companion. She savored the best of two very different worlds. She liked her life with her coyote mate. It was stimulating and exciting. At the same time, when the pendulum of her needs swung to the other extreme, she could flee her wild existence and rejoin her lifelong friend and the kind of man who soothed her her with gentle words and pans of nourishing food.

Happy and Wyn still shared an occasional hunting expedition. Schooled by her coyote mate, Wyn now took over as the superior hunter. Happy, too, soon learned the wild ways of tracking and hunting. Wyn led the hunt with a free, ranging stride that carried her swiftly and gracefully. Even eight weeks in whelp, she moved with ease, and her endurance now surpassed her companion's. Determined to keep pace, Happy pushed herself to prove an adequate hunting companion for Wyn.

* * * * *

The early June morning dawned crisp and clear. Its unusual chill invigorated the dogs. They had galloped off on a hunt before Will ever came outside. After covering many miles of mountain country, they stopped by a stream to drink and rest. Happy stretched out next to Wyn and dozed. During the entire morning, Wyn's coyote mate watched the two Newfoundlands from a safe distance. Although he did not join Wyn in her domestic life, he always knew where she was.

He waited patiently for a long time before he called to her. Wyn lifted her head when she heard him, then got up and trotted off in the direction of his voice. She found him standing behind a patch of dense shrubs, out of Happy's view. They greeted each other playfully and broke into a gentle game of chase. Hearing their scuffling, Happy was roused from her nap. Curious, she made her way toward the woods. When she found the pair, she stood motionless and watched them intently. Within moments, Wyn sent her mate tumbling, and he rolled to a stop almost directly under Happy's nose. He regained his feet immediately and met Happy's eyes for a brief moment. Then, in typical coyote style, he vanished silently into the brush.

Wyn watched him go, but decided not to chase after him. Instead, she returned to Happy whose attention was focused toward the brush that had swallowed up the coyote. Wyn sniffed Happy's muzzle as if to communicate that all was well. Still in a playful mood, she wagged her tail widely and nudged Happy with her body. At last, Happy focused on her companion, then bounded off playfully with Wyn following.

Quickly, the pair fell into a trot. Side by side, they resumed their journey in the general direction of the cabin. Happy looked back only once, but there was no sign of Wyn's wild companion.

Wyn's coyote had sensed no danger from his mate's placid friend. Still curious, he circled back now toward the dogs. He knew about the other dog at the cabin. He was aware that it was another female. This bit of knowledge, as much as anything, drew him back toward the two Newfoundlands. He slowed his pace once he located them, staying behind and observing carefully as they picked their way along the trail toward their mountain home. Still curious about the other female, he was drawn closer and closer to the pair. Finally, he could stand the tension no longer.

Wyn was aware of approaching movement only a split-second before a grey-brown streak blurred past her. Brushing quickly against Happy, the coyote darted away again into the bushes. Both dogs stopped, their heads up. Each sensed the excitement; neither felt fear. Wyn knew from a whiff of scent that the animal was her mate. She waited for his return in playful anticipation, her tail lifted high and waving. For a long time, neither dog moved. Both riveted their attention on the shrubs ahead where the hairy apparition had disappeared. Finally, they began to move on.

Suddenly, the coyote leaped from the high brush and bounced onto the trail, landing on all fours about ten feet in front of Happy. He remained visible for only an instant before leaping out of sight again. Wyn stopped. This time her tail wagged widely; she was ready to play. When the coyote returned again, she willingly joined him in a favorite game of leap and chase. Both Wyn and the coyote alternately appeared and disappeared.

At first Happy was bewildered by their leaping antics. Sometimes, just for an instant, she could see both animals. Then they vanished from view into the thicket, and she could only hear them as branches cracked. Then one or both would appear on the trail in full view.

The coyote had wisely calculated that this game would allow him an opportunity to get better acquainted with the other female. He was in control, and not at all vulnerable as he dashed in and out of her sight. At just the right moment, he leaped in front of Happy, materializing almost nose to nose with her. Then, before she had time to react, he was gone. Just as the coyote intended, Happy responded eagerly to his playfulness. She lifted her tail high and waved it in anticipation of play. When the coyote reappeared in front of her, she lowered her front legs to the ground in a pre-leap gesture that clearly communicated her playfulness.

Continuing the game, the coyote whizzed past Happy's muzzle and then vanished again into the cover of greenery. He repeated his quick reappearances two more times. Each time he nudged Happy and then disappeared. Each encounter was just a bit longer than the one before. Then Wyn joined in the game.

Delighted by their own improvisation, the three youthful friends teased, crouched and leaped in a bouncing game of chase. Their high spirits exploded in a series

155

of tumbles, sideways maneuvers, cautious step by step stalking, and an occasional high leap and twist in the air by the coyote. It was a great game among three energetic canines. Within a few minutes, however, it was all over. The wise young coyote felt confident now that Happy posed no threat to him; all he saw in those brown eyes was curiosity and playfulness. For her part, Happy was amused by the amber-eyed comic. She accepted him as a companion just as Wyn did.

Now that the game was over, the canines felt the need to meet formally. The coyote was alert and cautious, but he greeted Happy with a surface flamboyance, strolling up and touching noses, sniffing her face lightly. He moved off playfully, then came toward her again. This time, both animals sniffed each other, from muzzle to tails. Then, as if seized by a demon, the coyote took off in a burst of speed and disappeared, charged by the thrill of his success in meeting this new female. He had handled the encounter wisely, but now he felt a tremendous tension. He was not used to meeting females, but he sensed a strong, natural desire to add Happy to his family. He had traveled only a short distance before he regained control and stopped. After shaking vigorously as though to rid himself of the last vestige of immaturity, he turned and trotted confidently back to the two females.

Happy and Wyn watched as the coyote approached. He moved boldly, going first to Wyn and greeting her in his customary manner. She, in turn, responded, boosting his confidence. Next the young male turned to Happy, walking up to her with an air of supreme confidence. She stood watching with her head up and her tail lifted, alert to his approach. She liked his boldness. They touched muzzles, then he moved to her side and sniffed her carefully. She was enormous beside him. The coyote lifted a front paw to Happy's shoulder as if to mount her, then stood there for a moment with his body raised over her, announcing his position as a dominant male. Her big head turned toward him in acknowledgement of his behavior. She made no sound, but moved away from him; he dropped down to a stand beside her and did not try to mount her again. He was confident now that she was his.

The three companions resumed their journey. As they moved along, the coyote took extra time to mark his territory. This was a good day for him. He felt the bloom of full adulthood, traveling confidently with two females in his harem. For the moment, there was a compatible blending of the wild and the domestic. They were in the coyote's world now. But soon, the two females turned onto the trail that led back home, and he could not follow. He stopped and watched as they moved on without him, then yapped softly. Wyn looked back, but his insistence was fruitless. With careless abandon, they traveled on toward their domestic world of human friendship.

A natural fear of man held the young coyote at bay as his two black mates trotted up the trail, over the crest of the hill, past the chicken house, and down into the clearing. His sensitive ears heard the man's voice greet the dogs cheerfully. An occasional playful bark drew the coyote to the top of the ridge. All his senses told him that his mates were not afraid or in danger. But he had no experience to help him understand the rapport between dog and man. Intently, he watched as his new female rolled upside down so that the man could scratch her woolly underside. His mate, too, appeared glad to be with the man. But she and the man did not touch.

The coyote stayed for a long time, watching and learning. The sweet fragrance of good things to eat drifted to him as the man set pans of food down for the dogs. The coyote lifted his muzzle and sniffed lightly. He wasn't really hungry, but a thin line of saliva trailed from his mouth in response to the aroma. After the meal, the clearing became very quiet. Wyn stretched full-length on the ground near the porch step. One female hopped up on the porch, sat down next to the man and stretched her head into his lap. The last rays of sun slipped off the tops of the mountains. Then all was still.

Confused and uneasy, the coyote turned away from his black mates and moved back into his own wild world. He traveled with his feelings for a time, then stopped and expressed them in a single cry.

The sound drifted softly and plaintively to Wyn as she lay resting in the clearing. Her stomach was full, and she was content. But the voice drifting to her through the early evening darkness stirred her to her feet. She paced around the clearing, then moved to the top of the slope and stood for a long time, looking back at Will and Happy. Finally comfortable with her decision, she turned away from the cabin and all that it offered and slipped off at a trot into the darkness.

Will took the pipe from his mouth and tapped the

ashes onto the ground by the step, then leaned over and ruffled Happy's coat. She lay curled next to his foot, sleeping. Her warm presence comforted him. He, too, heard the lonely call of the coyote, and when Wyn disappeared into the darkness, he understood.

TWELVE

THE BIRTH

The cool darkness of the den comforted Wyn. She panted softly, got up, turned around, scratched at the soft earth beneath her, then lay down and panted again. Wyn had carried her pups easily for a full nine weeks. Now she could feel their strong bodies rebelling against the pressure of her muscles. But the time had come for the whelps to leave the warmth within their dam. Wyn was in labor.

This morning, she refused her breakfast. In the past weeks, Will had watched the big dog's sides swell. Her body carriage changed, she was pendulous with milk, and she'd dug some holes under some of the bushes at the edge of the clearing . . . all characteristic of fast-approaching motherhood. It surprised Will when she'd appeared this morning; she had been gone for two days. "Maybe she's come home to have those pups," he thought out loud as he set down her food. Wyn had looked back at him with drooping eyes. Later, as he picked up the untouched breakfast, he decided he'd better keep an eye on her.

Heading for the cabin, Will felt suddenly concerned. It surprised him that he cared so much; this was just a dog! But no, she was more. She was another being he had come to love and respect.

Will stood on the porch, drew in a deep breath, and exhaled heavily, then he turned his attention to Wyn once again. "Well, Black Dog," he said gently, "you pick your place. I think your time has come." His voice dropped to a throaty whisper.

Wyn stood and watched Will disappear into the cabin. She looked at Happy, who was busy eating her breakfast, and then turned away from the clearing. As if drawn by a magnet, she made her way to the den on the side of the hill. Feelings within her would not let her rest, but it felt good to be in the cool shadows of the den. Wyn's coyote mate knew she was there, and he did not go near. Both were content that all was as it should be. In their own ways, each waited for things to come.

As the hours passed, Wyn continued to pant and shift and dig. She moved in and out of the sheltered area. At the day's close she stood looking down over the valley below, rosy with the sunset's reflected glow. At last, she crawled back into the security of her den, lay down, and attempted to sleep. But the desire to dig moved her again. Without opening her eyes, she scraped several times at the dirt beneath her. But there were intriguing new scents on the ground. She stood and examined them carefully. They were just wet spots, but they puzzled her.

At this point in her labor, Wyn was perhaps more comfortable and better off than if she had whelped a planned Newfoundland litter in her kennel home. Here, in the wild, circumstances permitted her to proceed with the birthing ritual in a natural way. At home, she would have been limited to a whelping area and forced to cope with the activities of a hovering human. Instead, Wyn could experience the cool quiet of the natural shelter she and her mate had selected. Here, she found security. Here, she could respond to the natural instincts that had led her this far.

Wyn sniffed at the moisture on the den floor again. As she moved about in the shelter, she found the scent on her own body. Responding to instinct, she sniffed and washed herself carefully, then sniffed some more. Still panting quietly, she stretched out on her side. It felt good to change positions. Her whole body was at rest. She pushed her feet against one wall of the den, her back solidly against the opposite wall and breathed deeply. For a few moments she ceased panting. Deep within her body, all was ready. Wyn pushed against the wall with her feet. Her ribcage bulged briefly into a hardened ball, then relaxed. She breathed easily, resting quietly as the process continued. Again her muscles contracted. This time it lasted a bit longer. Time after time, the muscles worked to expel the first whelp. Totally at ease, Wyn labored and waited patiently. This new experience seemed as natural to her as all of her wild existence.

After a while, she felt the need to get up. With some effort, she stood and them made her way toward the open air. At the entrance of the little den, she stood for a short time, listening. Darkness had come to the mountain slope. Wyn walked a short distance from the entrance, emptied her bladder, and checked again under her tail, still pondering the strange odor. Another muscular contraction sent her hurrying back into the den. She crawled quickly into its safety, and again lay down with her back pressed firmly against the interior wall.

As the contractions continued, Wyn changed positions frequently. Occasionally, feeling the need to rearrange her nest, she scratched at the dirt beneath her. At last, all things were ready. She lay down flat on her chestbone; she arched her back, and with the next mighty effort of Wyn's muscles, a silvery mass appeared. Another strong push, and it slipped out onto the ground.

All was quiet. Her body was at rest. Wyn did not know at first that she had a whelp to care for. Not until she felt the little one squirming beneath her did she check to see what was there. She sniffed curiously, recognizing much the same smell as the fluids she'd found in her nest earlier. The tiny bundle kept moving. Wyn examined it again and made a tentative attempt to wash it with her tongue. Then, instinctively, she bit and nipped at it. The silvery casing broke, and a wet, squirming baby emerged. He lay there quietly, fluids spilling from around him, his wet sides expanding and contracting as he took in his first breaths of air.

Wyn sniffed the puppy carefully. With her sharp front teeth, she pulled and tugged on the cord. It shredded, separating the placenta from the pup. Quickly, Wyn

166

cleaned her nest of the ragged tissues, then turned her attentions to her new whelp. Despite her initial curiosity, Wyn's real interest in the puppy did not begin until he squeaked his first sounds. Then, instantly, she became a mother.

Wyn washed and tumbled her wavering baby, scrubbing him roughly from head to toe with a big pink tongue. He attempted to struggle toward her; she vigorously washed him away. Although his sounds were really complaints, Wyn didn't seem to mind. She brought her ears forward, happy and curious, when the little whelp practiced with his newfound voice. Then, inspired by his grunting, she washed him some more. Wyn's firstborn was strong and hungry. He staggered his way to her side, sniffling and rooting. Still washing him vigorously, Wyn pushed him away from her breast. But he struggled back to her side, persistent and determined, guided by powerful survival instincts.

As the young whelp battled his attentive mother for his first meal, Wyn's curious mate came closer to the den to investigate the new sounds and scents. There was a natural dictate that he should not come too close, and he obeyed his instincts. But he did not stray far from the den. These were new sounds and new scents he had never encountered before. They did not frighten him, but they gave him a feeling he did not understand. He lifted his voice in the darkness and announced his fatherhood. Then, he was silent.

Still absorbed with one another, neither Wyn nor her little one reacted to the midnight serenade. The struggling, hungry whelp continued his guttural protests, but he was no match in strength for his mother's enduring attention. Once more, Wyn's powerful muscles began to work. Distracted now from the pup, she gave in again and again to the demanding pressures forcing her next whelp into its new life.

Wyn began caring for the second pup even before it was fully born, sniffing and washing the little legs that stretched and pawed at the new environment. As its head emerged, the new pup's squeaky little voice gurgled with fluids. At the moment of birth, Wyn greeted it with an able and experienced tongue. Wash and tumble, wash and tumble . . . the same sequence that had greeted her firstborn male. This one, a female, was as strong and determined as her brother, and a great deal more vocal. It didn't take her long to squeak out a long, high-pitched protest. Already, the tremendous drive to find food had her wobbling on newborn legs, straining to find the warm satisfaction of a meal. Yet, against all protests, the young mother continued to tumble and roll her new puppy.

This time, Wyn snipped the cord deftly with her teeth, then quickly disposed of the remaining tissues. Once satisfied her nest was clean, she lifted the whelp in her mouth and placed it between her front legs. Here she found good control. With the little female trapped by her mother's persistent scrubbing, the male finally found the opportunity to seek food uninterrupted.

Wyn's firstborn had emerged equipped with many survival instincts. His little legs were strong enough to get him to his mother's side. His head and mouth were oversized, equipped to extract the milk that would make him grow strong. Searching by scent for the sweet aroma of his first milk, the puppy sucked instinctively at his mother's side. Not at all by accident, he found a fragrant teat and, fumbling, drew it into his mouth. Unsure how to control the abundant flow, he choked and sputtered a bit at first, then finally began to fill his deep need for food.

Squeaking in protest, the little female continued battling her mother's unrelenting tongue. Her brother had been far more willing to accept Wyn's attention than this spunky, vocal female. Unfortunately for her, there was no sibling arriving soon to distract Wyn from her mothering.

Occasionally Wyn left the female whelp just long enough to sniff the male, now busy tugging away at her breast and mewing with contentment. The hungry pup quit sucking, but held on tightly while Wyn washed his face; then, he resumed nursing more vigorously than before. Already, he knew to press and stretch to help release the sweet liquid, and his little paws pushed hard against Wyn's body.

Content at last that her squirming female was properly clean, Wyn finally let her go. Nuzzling through her mother's neck coat and under her front leg, the little whelp eventually found her way to her brother. The inviting scents were strong there, and she struggled for his place. But the little male was almost an hour older than his new sister and much stronger. He held his space, and the little female moved on in her frantic attempt to find food. At last, near Wyn's back leg, she succeeded in attaching herself to a full, easy-flowing teat, and her struggling ceased. She drew in the rich fluid easily. As the next hour passed, the two dark little bodies swelled into plump, shining shapes. They were now dry, warm, and full of milk.

Wyn rested as her babies nursed. The sensation was a pleasant one. She was content in her den home with her little family tugging away at her. Resting comfortably with her little ones, she did not even move during the next two contractions. Then her instincts set her in motion again. She sniffed over the newborns. The male was sleeping. The female was still fitfully nursing.

Wyn gave in easily to each contraction, stretching full length and letting the muscles do their work. Occasionally, she moved her body slightly to a new position, then rested again. At last, another shining membrane bulged from her body. A final thrust forced the wet mass onto the den floor.

Immediately, Wyn pushed with her hind legs to back her body away from the two older whelps, giving herself easy access to the newest pup without endangering the others. As she moved to tend the squirming sac, they quickly snuggled close to their mother again, still leaving Wyn in an easy position to take care of the new arrival. Expertly, Wyn tore away the tissues and began washing the pup, turning it with her tongue. Again the magic of the newborn's tiny sounds drew her ears forward in pleasure. She had never looked more beautiful than in these first moments of new motherhood.

Strong and vigorous, the new whelp struggled against Wyn's big pink tongue. But she cleaned him thoroughly, feeling his strength as he resisted her. Finding the placenta still attached to his body, she stretched and shredded it until it separated from him, then severed the cord with one quick nip. A gush of blood spurted into Wyn's mouth and over her muzzle. As the pup moved, the red stream arched up and across her eyes. She blinked and shook her head, then went back to work. But the blood kept flowing. Wyn had severed the cord too close to the pup's body.

As with the others, Wyn gave the new whelp a thorough scrubbing, then allowed him to try nursing while she quickly checked over the rest of her family. Satisfied that all was clean, she returned to the new male and again washed his belly. Her tongue moved quickly over the rest of his little body, under his tail, around his neck and muzzle, and back to the bleeding cord.

Then, with a caring sniff at each of the other newborns, she stretched out on her side in the den, giving the pups easy access to nurse. The soft light of early morning cast a gentle glow over Wyn and her new family. She felt comfortable. The firstborn was sound asleep next to her, his little stomach full and round. The little female still stirred occasionally into fitful moments of nursing. Now, the third tugged at Wyn's breast, giving her a pleasant sensation. Each sound from her little ones seemed good and satisfying to Wyn. This was her reward for being a good mother.

Wyn felt overcome by a strong desire to sleep. Once more, she washed the still bleeding belly of the newest whelp. She felt his tugs at her breast, gave a final lick to his face, and then put her head down on the soft earth. One deep breath, and she was asleep.

171

The blood continued to drain from the newest male. Its spurting had subsided now to a gentle flow, and the whelp's strength began to diminish. His drive for food ebbed along with his blood until, finally, his mouth slipped from the teat. Without the desire to struggle for food, he rested, warm and untroubled within the soothing rhythm of his mother's breathing. Wyn slept on innocently as her little family dwindled to two.

THIRTEEN

A NEW HOME

The June morning sunlight could not penetrate into the depths of the den, but the sounds of birds drifted to Wyn's ears and roused her. Although she had slept only a few hours, she felt rested. Immediately, she turned to her little ones. All three lay nestled together at her side. She washed each in turn. Life for the young whelps seemed a constant struggle for food against the force of the giant pink tongue. The first male got a gentle tumbling and complete morning bath from head to toe. Then the little female was rudely awakened and rolled from side to side. When Wyn came to the third pup, the little form was cold. Curious, she sniffed it and nudged it with her nose. She sniffed the ground where it lay. Then she nudged it again, and after a final sniff, rolled it away from the nest. She showed no concern over the cold little body. Though she did not understand, instinct told her that this object did not belong in the nest. She pushed it again, this time as far as she could move it toward the den opening without getting up.

Wyn turned her attention to the two remaining pups who were now tugging away at her with eager mouths. She carefully examined the little male, then his squeaking litter mate. More gently now, she tended each one anew. She snuffled, then washed, then snuffled again. A sweet, caring expression brightened her face, prompted by the sounds of her little family. Wyn was a good mother. She was totally devoted to the husky pair of babies kneading at her breasts with their tiny paws.

After letting the young ones nurse a while longer, Wyn felt the need to get up and empty herself. She stood, letting the suckling whelps drop gently back to the den floor. Again she went over them meticulously with her muzzle, then gingerly moved toward the entrance, taking great care not to step on her pups. On her way out of the den, she stopped and sniffed the cold little form, then picked it up in her mouth and crawled out into the daylight.

Wyn blinked at the mid-morning sun. The air was warm. She felt free and light as she moved from the den, still carrying the dead whelp in her mouth. She put it down, moved a few steps away and relieved herself on a clump of grass. The thought of water at the foot of the hill drew her in that direction. She took only a few steps, then turned back to pick up the tiny body. Lifting it gently in her mouth, she began her trek down the hill.

Wyn had no definite feeling about what to do with the dead pup. It was indecision that convinced her to keep it with her for a time. Repeatedly, she put it down, walked away from it, then returned to it again. At last, just before she got to the stream, she turned to one side of the downhill path and deposited the small form by a shrub. With her nose she attempted to cover it with dirt, then, overcome with a driving urge for water, she turned away from her dead whelp and hurried down the hill to quench her thirst.

Wading into the cool water, Wyn drank, enjoying the feeling of the water trickling down her throat. She stood for a time with her feet and legs in the flow of the stream, drank some more and then turned back up the hill. Part way up the trail, she met the coyote. They wagged a greeting, and he examined her with his nose, evaluating the unusual odors that were now a part of his mate. Following her back toward the den, he stopped before they reached the entrance. Wyn didn't even look back. The closer she got to the nest, the faster she moved. She disappeared quickly through the black opening.

With a great sense of security and contentment, the new mother stepped carefully over her pups and lay down with them. They were sleeping, but their little noses could tell them what their eyes could not see. They knew she was back. And now, not yet one day old, instinct drew them back to their mother's side where they could nurse freely.

The next day, Wyn returned from the stream without meeting the coyote. She had become so accustomed to seeing him there that she looked around for him. Back at the den, she paused and looked once more. But he was not there. Wyn turned and disappeared into her nursery. Not long after she had settled in with her family, Wyn heard the coyote at the den entrance. He gave a soft yap, a familiar communication between them. This was the first time the young father had been bold enough to come near the den since the pups were born. Wyn listened, her ears alert, straining to determine if he were still there. She tested the air, and her nose told her he was there. She sniffed again, and another scent came to her. It was a warm animal smell.

Once again the coyote yapped to her softly. He left his offering at the den entrance and trotted off about twenty feet to lie down and watch. The aroma of food drifted to Wyn on a warm current of morning air. As her hungry young ones tugged and kneaded at her, for the first time since whelping, Wyn felt the need for food for herself. Again, the warm tantalizing aroma drifted invitingly to her. She sniffed the air, lifting her muzzle to gain every bit of fragrant scent that she could. She knew there was a rabbit out there. She began to salivate; a few drops fell on her front legs. She was hungry.

Wyn stood carefully, stepped over her squeaking, protesting young ones, and moved toward the entrance. She was cautious at first, as though stalking prey. As she moved closer to the opening, the aroma grew stronger. Another step or two, and she saw the rabbit just outside the opening to the den where her mate had left it. It was still; it did not run. She did not have to stalk, chase and kill her first meal since the birth of the pups. It was waiting for her.

Focusing on the food, Wyn crawled out of the den and grabbed the rabbit. She moved a few feet away before she lay down with it in her front of her. She tore away eagerly at its middle section, devouring the precious food so necessary for her to continue feeding her young. In a short time, most of the rabbit had disappeared. Bits and pieces were all that remained. Wyn stood. She licked her jaws and washed one front leg.

The coyote watched from his vantage point without moving or calling attention to himself. Only after Wyn was on her feet did he stand and move toward her. At that moment, a large shadow enveloped them, causing the coyote to flinch and dart for the safety of a thicket by the stream. In the same instant, Wyn charged to the den entrance to check her pups. A golden eagle had glided by on the air currents above the two canines, stirring their primeval fears.

For the coyote, the threat was immediate and acute, but easily shrugged off as quickly as the shadow vanished from his domain. Not so with Wyn. Her whole being now was enveloped by the responsibilities of motherhood. The incident heightened her awareness of the dangers to her young and caused her protective instincts to peak. Still tense, Wyn quaked inside as she stood over her young and faced the den opening, ready to protect them should an intruder come too close.

Engulfed by her fear for the pups, she stood without moving for many minutes. Gradually her concern lessened, her body relaxed, and the squealing demands of the tiny female drew her back to the reality of more pressing duties. Wyn moved to the entrance and checked her territory for danger. It was gone. And so was her mate.

Reassured for the moment, she returned to her tottering infants. Always hungry, they greeted her with bobbing heads as she curled around them. Wyn breathed a deep sigh and listened to the pups gurgle and gulp her rich milk. She did not sleep. There were new feelings simmering within her now, and her brown eyes were fixed on the entrance to the den.

During the next few days, Wyn remained constantly with her young, leaving the den only for the basic necessities. She had a good supply of water available, and her mate brought enough food to satisfy her appetite. Occasionally, she met briefly with her coyote by the stream, but her time was completely consumed by a desire to care for her fast-growing pups. All the while, she was aware of a discontent growing within her.

When the pups were five days old, Wyn responded to her instincts. She was no longer bound to stay with them all the time. She took a few rest periods just outside the den entrance. Here she could look out over the valley, breathe the fresh air and enjoy some freedom from her young family. Strange odors within the den bothered Wyn each time she returned from outside. She felt more and more strongly that she must move her young.

On the morning of the sixth day, Wyn came outside, went to the stream for a drink, and instead of returning to her resting place outside the den, took off on a short hunt. As a nursing mother, she had a constant need for food. Wyn knew this territory well. She knew where to find food.

The season's young were now half-grown rabbits and ground squirrels. Still ignorant of clever survival tactics, they made easy prey. Wyn made a pass through the area where she had first lived on the mountain. She deliberately sought out the rock ledge where she had healed with Happy's care after her encounter with the rancher. The area was just as she remembered it. She still felt secure here on the ledge. It was protected, quiet and cool. Wyn sniffed around carefully. There were no animal smells. The ledge was unused. After a thorough investigation, she turned and, breaking into a trot, headed straight for her pups.

Wyn hurried into the nest without hesitation. Carefully, she sniffed over each baby and washed them in her usual tumbling fashion. She had never been gone from her family for such a long time, and she was glad to be back with them again. Stretching out on her side, she gave the pups free access to nurse, much as she would if she had a large litter to feed. The young pups now nursed from one teat to another, taking only those that offered a fast, abundant supply. Already, they had doubled their size since birth.

Thirst woke Wyn after a long sleep. She stretched. Her movements jostled the sleeping pups. They stretched too, then snuggled close to her and continued to sleep. Wyn moved away from them, crawled out of the den and stood quietly listening to the sounds of the evening. Faintly in the distance she heard a coyote call, and then another answered. She could tell neither was her mate. As the sounds faded, she made her way down to the stream.

As she was drinking, the coyote joined her. They walked, trotted, and played a bit on the stream banks. Their spirits were high. Wyn waded into the trickling water to drink again, then turned and invited him to play some more. He was quick to respond. They cavorted and splashed, jumped and pounced. And then suddenly, Wyn's mood changed.

She hopped up on the bank and shook herself free of the water, moved a short distance, then stopped and looked back. The coyote was standing by the water's edge looking at her. In a moment, he was bouncing after her; in response, she again broke into a trot, heading away from the den. The coyote followed. Together they traveled the mile from the den to the ledge Wyn knew so well. The coyote could smell evidence of Wyn's visit earlier in the day. It was almost dark; together, the two of them left the ledge and returned to their little family.

Wyn took charge of the activities. She disappeared into the den and came out again with a pup in her mouth. It was squirming and grunting, struggling against her big jaws. She put it down only long enough to get a firm and gentle grip. Then, with the puppy held securely in place, she headed off in the direction of her old ledge home. Her curious mate followed. He still felt no need to take part in the care of the young ones, but he was attentive to Wyn. He wanted to understand what she was doing.

Still haunted by the presence of the hunter in the sky, Wyn needed to find a place where she felt her pups would be safe. Instinct drove her to move them from their birth place.

The ledge offered a haven of security now, as it had

when she was injured. With the safety of her pups being her only goal, she would not rest until they were away from the den of shadows. As far as Wyn was concerned, it was merely an accident that her mate was around for the proceedings. With or without his sanction, she had to move her pups.

Still carrying the pup firmly in her jaws, Wyn made her way around the path that led to the ledge. She lowered her head and moved to the back section of the shelter where there was barely room for her to stand. Carefully, she lowered the squirming pup to the soft earth. He grunted a complaint. Indifferent to his protests, Wyn sniffed at him. With a strong sense of satisfaction, she polished him with her pink tongue and stood over him for a long moment. Then, as if on sudden impulse, she turned and disappeared, hurrying back to the den where the little female pup waited alone.

The coyote followed Wyn as she traveled to the ledge with the first pup in her mouth, and he watched her leave the ledge without it. His growing curiosity drove him around the path and into the depths of the ledge home. Gingerly, he walked up to the youngster. The pup lifted his sightless face toward his sire and sniffed the new smell in this strange place. He felt the muzzle sniff him all over, his head, his belly, around his tail. The tiny grunting thing on the dirt held the coyote in a momentary spell. It faintly smelled of his mate, yet it wasn't. He could find no way to communicate with it. Puzzled, he backed away, beginning to feel that this was no place for him.

The young father retreated quickly from the ledge, and from the odd creature he'd found there. He tingled with strange feelings stimulated by the smell of the tiny body, so different, yet so like his mate. He felt compelled to stay near the pup, yet he struggled with a desire to follow Wyn. In the darkness, he heard sounds of an approaching animal.

It was Wyn, coming over the rise with the second pup in her mouth. The little female was much more adamant in her protests about being moved. She stretched her tiny body in an attempt to free herself, but the jaws held her in a firm and relentless grip. Still protesting her plight, she joined her brother in their new home.

The little male was still awake, mounded silently against the back wall of the ledge when Wyn arrived. Gently, she put the second pup down and sniffed a greeting to the male before subjecting the testy female to the inevitable bath. The pups drew close to each other as she nuzzled them. Her presence comforted them in this place full of strange new scents. They nursed, relaxed and slept.

Wyn rested far into the night without sleeping. Her head was up, her ears alert, assessing the different sounds of her new den. She sounded one "woof" into the darkness; it brought back a quiet response. Wyn knew that her mate was there.

Wyn was at peace in this shelter that had served her well in a time of desperate need. She had removed her pups from the strange odors of their birthing room and the shadowy warnings of predators.

Just before dawn, Wyn relaxed, stretching full-length within the comfortable confines of her old ledge home. She knew her pups would be safe here.

FOURTEEN

THE VISIT

Even in mid-June, morning dawned cool on the mountain. The night's storm had cleared the air so that the distant mountains seemed close enough to touch from the cabin steps. Happy was awake and content. Stretched out on the porch, she tested the morning air, then hopped down and ambled over to the pump for a drink. She shook herself and sniffed the air again. The crispness of the new day filled her with an overwhelming desire to run. She dashed around the yard in circles, came to a sudden halt, then dashed off again. The antic feeling surging through her body reflected in her eyes. Feeling as lighthearted as a pup, Happy ran over the top of the hill, past the chicken house, and into the forest.

Galloping through her mountain homeland, the big dog made a dash at two startled squirrels, but she was not in the mood for a hunt. With the chill air fueling her energies, she was merely responding to the joy of being alive and free. Soon, however, her size and weight slowed her to a fast trot. But her feeling of well-being did not diminish in the least.

As she moved easily through the familiar woodlands, Happy crossed a scent that brought her to an abrupt halt. She whirled, and her nose went down to investigate. Quickly, she found it. Here, suddenly and unexpectedly, was strong evidence that Wyn had passed this way not long ago. Responding to instinct that tells animals which way the trail leads, Happy set off to find her friend.

There was an urgency in her purpose now. She followed Wyn's scent easily, as though it was a white line painted through the forest. Where Wyn had veered from the trail, Happy did also. She did not lift her head as she followed the scent. No activity in the grasses or brush attracted her attention. Her single purpose was to find Wyn. Never wavering from the evidence that her companion was somewhere near, she settled into a slow trot.

Happy was fully aware that she was nearing the familiar territory surrounding the ledge where she and Wyn had spent so much time during the winter. As she came nearer, the scent intensified, and her pace quickened. She was going to find Wyn!

In her eagerness, Happy charged the final steps up the path to the ledge, then slid to a stop just inside the ledge entrance, face to face with a startled, protective mother who greeted the intruder with bared fangs and a threatening growl. Immediately, Happy lifted her head slightly and turned her gaze to one side to defuse the unpleasant encounter. She retreated a step, then held her position.

LIVE OAK

The moment she recognized Happy, Wyn relaxed her vicious warning. Still wary, however, she covered her pups with her big head, eyed Happy suspiciously and rumbled a slow warning. Obediently, Happy slowly backed away from Wyn and the pups, then turned to the path and quickly made her way out of Wyn's sight. When she felt she was a safe distance away, Happy sat down and watched the entrance to the ledge. She was puzzled.

It was not long before Wyn appeared. Although Happy had just invaded the privacy of her nest, she had recovered quickly from the shock. Wyn wanted to see her companion. It had been two weeks since they had been together.

The bond between the Newfoundlands remained steadfast. Genuinely glad to see one another, they touched muzzles and wagged their tails widely. As long as Happy did not come too close to Wyn's young family, the two dogs could maintain their easy friendship. Gradually time would ease Wyn's anxieties, and she would relax her guarded care. But for now any socializing between the two long-time friends would take place away from the pups.

Happy was curious about the new smells of Wyn's body. Cautiously at first, she approached Wyn to sniff. As though she understood Happy's feelings, Wyn stood still for the inspection. When Happy had satisfied her curiosity, she picked up a large stick and shook it in Wyn's face, wagging her tail in expectation. It was one of their favorite games . . . keep-away.

For a short and joyous time, Wyn obliged her friend.

The two dogs crouched and leaped at one another. They ran and rolled on the ground, playing together as they had all of their lives. All too quickly, however, playtime was over. Wyn's maternal drive sent her back to a post near the entrance to her nest. She lay down there, still wagging her tail, and refused to move.

During their two weeks of separation, Wyn had been preoccupied with her maternal duties. The reunion with Happy was comforting to her. She felt the same security now that she had when Happy nursed her back to health months ago. More than an hour passed before the two companions ended their quiet interlude together.

Finally, hunger stirred Happy to her feet. She walked over to Wyn and sniffed her muzzle, then trotted away from the ledge. As she started for the cabin, it was her assumption that Wyn would follow. Much to her surprise, that did not happen. She stopped and waited for a moment at the top of the rise behind the ledge, sensing the differences in Wyn, but not able to understand. Then hunger nudged her again, and she turned and trotted home.

Wyn stood at the entrance to her den and watched her friend leave. A mixture of feelings gathered within her. She waited, but Happy did not return. After a few minutes, she moved to the crest of the hill above, in time to see her companion lengthen the distance between them and disappear. With a sigh, Wyn turned and hurried back to her little family, while Happy trotted home to Will, content with the events of her morning.

THE PACK

During the days that followed, Happy returned to the ledge frequently to spend time with Wyn. She was always greeted with a quiet growl that excluded her from the intimacy of the den's interior. Its sounds and smells aroused Happy's curiosity, but Wyn had set limits, and she respected them.

The pups were healthy and growing. Although their hazy blue eyes had been open since they were ten days old, their vision was still developing. They saw very little, even when they fixed their gaze in the direction of sound or movement. The protected cavern that was their den further limited their view. As the hours and the days slipped by, they ate and slept and tussled in a dim world. Rolling and tumbling, pulling relentlessly on each other's ears, they wrestled together in early attempts at puppy dominance that occasionally escalated into snarling squabbles.

Wyn spent time away only when it was necessary to hunt for food. When she returned, she always approached the ledge quietly and sniffed over her offspring. If it was not time to nurse them, she quickly took up her position on guard near the entrance. There she could protect her family from intruders and yet be free of their demands: for when she was near them she became an object of constant puppy amusement.

★ ★ ★ ★ ★

Although the coyote did not yet help in caring for the pups, he continued to bring Wyn food to supplement her short hunts. And frequently he found his way to the cabin area where he lured Happy away for a romp in the woods. His energy appealed to her. She found him a constant challenge to her playful nature. Although she was quite agile, the coyote could outmaneuver her at every turn. She could catch rabbits and squirrels with relative ease, but she could not capture her elusive companion in play. The coyote's play with Happy followed an entirely different pattern than with Wyn. Each female determined what games were played, and their wild friend was adaptable enough to respond.

Frustrated by her inability to tag her coyote playmate, Happy finally threw herself down and rolled on her back, with all four feet in the air. Squirming and growling, she tried to catch her tail. This playful antic always served as an invitation for the prankster coyote to attack. He loved to grab her by the thick hair of her neck and try to pull her around in the dirt, while she growled in playful protest. When Happy tired of the game, she jumped to her feet and ran in silly circles. The coyote's response was to dodge and attack repeatedly. These raucous sessions usually ended with Happy's flopping on the cool earth, exhausted.

Occasionally, all three canines hunted together, but Happy was more dependent now on Will's handouts than on game, so she was not driven with the same need for food as the coyote and Wyn. Some days, Happy traveled the woods alone. She loved to search out small creatures and chase after them, often without any real intent to catch them. She knew where many of the little animals lived and planned her treks to include those areas.

On one such occasion, a sound in the leaves drew Happy's attention. Quickly she stopped and turned a quizzical face toward the sound. The rustle came again. With typical curiosity, she approached the spot and pawed the leaves. Out hopped a huge toad. Happy nosed after it in amusement, her tail up, flagging her delight.

She had often played with toads on the lawn of her kennel home, unable to resist the grotesque toys with their bulging eyes and gorged bellies. She caught this one up in her mouth like a ball. Instantly, froth came bubbling from her mouth and dripped onto the ground. The toad had released a bitter fluid designed to revolt her and cause its release. Happy might have expected this unpleasant sensation from her previous experiences, but she had never learned. It was as though she knew what the outcome would be, but judged the capture worth the discomfort. She quickly spat out the toad and shook her head. It drew itself tightly into a ball and sat very still. Happy moved a few steps away, sat down and watched patiently. After a time, the toad unfolded itself, took a few awkward steps and then two great hops. Immediately, Happy was upon it once more, trying to harass it into more activity. But the toad refused to co-operate further, and Happy finally lost interest. At last, the big toad was safe to go on its way unharmed. Happy turned for home. That night, the meal from Will's kitchen took the bitter taste from her mouth.

By the time the pups were four weeks old, they were accustomed to spending most of their time alone. While the adults were gone, the two pups entertained them-selves with their own variations of juvenile games and practice battles. As they grew older, their curiosity grew as well. Each day they extended the distance they dared to travel from the inner confines of the ledge.

One morning, just as the pups had settled in beside Wyn to enjoy their morning meal, she quickly got up again. Still nursing, the pups hung on with frantic deter-mination. Wyn dragged them a short distance before they released their grip on her. Leaving them wide awake and still hungry, she stepped carefully over them, then moved out into the morning sun.

The young female stumbled after her mother for a few steps, but stopped at the opening of the den. Her big brother ambled up from behind her, and together they stood looking out into the bright morning. Their noses quivered as they sniffed for indications of their

Thistle

dam, but she was gone. The female pup took a few brave steps forward. She had never ventured beyond the den's entrance, but her curiosity was growing. The male pup came up to flank her, giving her the courage to move forward out into the open.

She was born a leader. She possessed a drive and an insatiable curiosity that carried her forward. Now, she stretched her neck and sniffed. Her mother's scent still lingered in the air. Again, the male pup came up beside her, and again she moved forward. This time, her brother sat and watched. He was not ready to move out into the unknown world. When the little female realized that he was not coming with her, she moved only a little farther ahead. All at once, she reached her outer limits, and her courage disintegrated rapidly. As though she was being chased by a demon, she scampered back under the ledge.

Her big brother watched in amusement. As she scurried back into the safety of her home, he pounced on her heavily. The little female let out a high-pitched yelp of surprise and terror, then unleashed a frenzied counterattack. Snarling and snapping, she bit hard into his face with sharp teeth. Bravely, the male accepted her retaliation, then with a quiet warning growl, he knocked her to the ground and pinned her with his greater strength. The female complained furiously, but he remained over her. Eventually she wilted under his relentless determination and stopped squealing. Only then did he release her and step back, his tail wagging. The tussle was over.

Eventually, the young female's temper and fears

quieted, and she settled herself for more ventures into the world beyond the den entrance. Each attempt took her farther. Each attempt gave her courage to try again. And each time the male waited behind and playfully attacked her when she returned to his chosen realm close by the den. Both pups were soon exhausted by their first morning of play at the den door.

The sunshine outside their dark home was a new sensation. Warm and penetrating like the warmth of their mother, it soothed their tired little bodies. Stretching out in patches of forest light, they slept soundly.

Comparing the sleeping pups, it was not difficult to tell male from female. They were the same color, black with tinges of silver and tan, but upon closer observation they were quite different. There was a greater breadth and massiveness to the male puppy. His short, round muzzle, his massive head and his deep chest all hinted of his Newfoundland heritage. All of these characteristics contrasted markedly with the delicate features already evident in his sister. Her slight skull, slender legs and chiseled features all carried the mark of her sire. And her ears seemed extremely large for her tiny head. But, like her coyote father, what she lacked in size, she made up for in her zest for life.

Suddenly, the pups' morning nap was interrupted by a sound. Until now, their life inside the den had insulated them from many of the natural sounds of the forest. This new stimulus frightened them. The little female was on her feet quickly. She scurried to the safety of the inner ledge, with her brother close behind.

Fully alert now, she tried to determine what had

awakened her. From her place of security, she turned to face the sound and woofed uneasily. Despite her tiny size, she exhibited all the behaviors of an adult canine on alert.

In a moment, Wyn appeared at the entrance to the den. The youngsters ran to greet her. She knew by scent that the two had been beyond the den entrance. Sniffing the area briefly, she explored their boldness and then stood over them as they scrambled to finish the meal denied them earlier. They sat on little haunches, supporting their front feet against her. Drinking noisily, they kneaded her methodically with their paws to help release the rich and abundant breakfast she still willingly offered.

Wyn stood patiently, her body relaxed and her head lowered nearly to the ground. A bit of saliva dripped from her mouth. Then, in a single contraction of her stomach, she deposited a soft mass of partially digested food on the ground. Suddenly and deliberately, she stepped away from her nursing young. Still clamoring for food, they struggled to reach her, but she pulled away again, intentionally separating herself from the hungry youngsters. For the first time, she was refusing to nurse them. Instead, she had provided them with their first solid food.

Catching the scent of the food, the female pup showed curiosity. She investigated it thoroughly with her nose, touched it lightly with her paw and again with her tongue to sample the taste. The experience was pleasing to her. The texture and aroma of the warm meal met certain innate needs in the little canine. Hungrily, she

202

licked, then finally bit and gulped her new food, driven by her appetite to eat more and more.

Wyn left the pair and disappeared from the ledge. The bewildered male pup watched her departure. He wanted more milk.

Then sounds behind him drew his attention. He turned to see his sister busy with the food. Curiosity drew him closer as his nose explored the new aroma. But as he put his mouth down to sample the meal, the female attacked him viciously, driving him back. By now, she was gulping ravenously. His approach, triggered a basic instinct. Again and again, the male approached. Each time, his sister's snarling fury drove him away. Finally, when she could hold no more, she relented and allowed the male to join her. With deliberation, he sampled the meal. Then he, too, gulped down the new nourishment, finding it just as satisfying and enjoyable as did his sister.

After both pups had gorged themselves, they waddled outside the entrance to the den, their sides bulging. They tried to lie down and sleep, but it took time to find a comfortable position. The female had eaten more than her share. Now she lay groaning and stretching. Long after her brother was sleeping peacefully, his sister was still paying the price for her gluttony. She stretched and belched and changed positions. At last, her stomach gave up a part of her overindulgence. Then, feeling more comfortable, she wandered over near her sleeping brother and soon she, too, lay sleeping soundly in the morning sun.

The coyote trotted up the slope toward the den. The

sun beamed hot on his back as he was headed for the shade of a dense shrub he had adopted as his outpost. He was almost upon the pups before he realized their presence. Their scent brought him to an abrupt halt only a short distance away. He was immobilized. The familiar scents of the den were partly Wyn and partly scents he associated with Wyn without fully understanding their origin. But now he sensed their presence in the two tiny black forms drowsing in the filtered sun.

Drawn by curiosity, the coyote moved a silent step closer and stretched his neck forward to gather more information. For some time now, he had heard sounds coming from the inner den, sounds he somehow connected with the new scents. Now, at last, he could see the source of these strange signals. Silently, he moved between the pups, eagerly investigating each one. As he brushed the female's tiny whiskers, she sneezed into wakefulness.

Her squeal of panic brought Wyn from a short distance away. She appeared on the scene just as the female pup scuttled for the safety of the den, her little tail tucked tightly between her legs. Big brother responded more slowly, sneaking a last backward glance at the large intruder who had disrupted his nap. But he, too, disappeared quickly into the dark security of his home.

Wyn greeted her mate with a tail wag. He acknowledged her presence with a quick glance, then moved a step closer to the den's entrance, still curious about the pups. His pups. Wyn passed him and entered the softly lit den to check on her youngsters. Her presence reassured them, but they did not follow her when she rejoined the coyote at the den entrance. Contented, Wyn flopped down in the afternoon sun.

The young sire's attention remained riveted on the opening to the den where he could see two shadowy forms sitting close together. Their mutual contact gave the pups courage to face the large creature who had suddenly appeared in their lives. As they watched him, he gradually seemed less fearsome. Wyn's unconcerned presence bolstered their resolve. The little female woofed nervously, but the intruder did not respond. With curiosity now tugging at her, the pup inched forward a little and woofed again. Still, the intruder remained silent. But this time his tail wagged. Seeing her dam lying close by inspired the little female with a hint of bravery. She moved forward again, finally edging out into the open. Now she felt a surge of fearlessness. Step by step, she made her way toward the coyote. Her brother remained behind.

At last, stretching forward, the young female touched her nose to the coyote's, then dashed away, scrambled over Wyn and sat peering at the coyote from behind her mother.

The coyote took in the entire incident with amusement. Although these creatures were no longer the small bodies Wyn had carried from their original home, his sense of kinship toward them welled within him, and he liked the feeling.

SIXTEEN

REAL DANGER

The summer days were peaceful ones for Wyn, the coyote and the pups. Occasionally, Happy joined the group and shared in the social upbringing of the youngsters. For short periods, she enjoyed their antics and rough attention. When she'd had enough of their playful pranks and flying attacks, she growled a soft warning and withdrew to a more distant resting place. Without ever hurting the pups, Happy could deliver an ultimatum that was accepted even by the young female. The pups learned quickly that she was part of the family circle, yet not always interested in their capers.

Occasional thunder showers sent the pups scurrying back to the safety of the ledge where they sat and looked out into the deluge with curiosity. Always the bold one, the little female tried darting out into the shower. She hunched down as if to escape the drenching feeling and then scuttled back to the protection of the den. As soon as the rain dwindled to sprinkles, both pups hurried back out into the open. With great leaps and splashes, they attacked the puddles, reveling in the luxury of cool water right at their front door. In their excitement, spontaneous wrestling matches were inevitable. Soon they were two dripping wet puppies.

The three-month-old pups had grown leggy and agile. They still spent most of their time close to the ledge, but gradually extended their range of adventure on frequent short explorations. Happy's aloofness eased as the two pups grew. Now, with calm acceptance, she joined Wyn and the coyote in submitting to the youngster's outrageous antics. At times, the adults even initiated games with the pups.

As they neared four months of age, their adult teeth began to replace needle-sharp baby teeth, rendering their mock attack much less painful.

Individuals from the start, the two siblings remained as different in personality as their sire and dam were in appearance. The little female exhibited all of the wild characteristics endowed by her heritage. Spirited and dominant, alert and inquisitive, she was full of drive and curiosity. Destined for adventure, she already exhibited a sense of fearlessness, coupled with the native intelligence that would give her the upper hand in many of life's encounters.

The male was soft and sweet like his mother and already exhibited many Newfoundland qualities. Although tempered in size by his sire's genes, he would grow much larger than the coyote. Despite his puppy squabbles with his sister, he was by nature quiet and

210

peaceful, willing in any situation to wait and watch, to assess and then act. His decisions were usually good.

Despite her attachment to the canine family group, Happy remained loyal to Will. After one particular morning with the pups and their parents, her needs for human companionship began to gnaw at her. She was restless and moved from spot to spot. Finally, consumed by the need to be with Will, she stood, shook, and without ceremony started for Will's home.

As usual, Happy checked each rustle of leaves or snapping twig along the way. Usually, she could tell what caused the sound by scent. Hunger did not drive her to investigate, but curiosity did. She couldn't resist an occasional game of chase with another four-footed creature, so she remained alert for any possibilities. There it was! A sound in the leaves nearby caught her attention. She turned to pinpoint its direction, but all was still again. Although there was no evidence of a squirrel or rabbit, she knew something was near.

Always curious, she approached the area cautiously. Again she heard the sound. It was clearly different from the usual forest sounds, just a rustling of leaves. Then a movement on the ground caught her attention. The muscular heap of a rattlesnake bunched in protest before the intruder. Lifting its head, the snake poised, facing her, its tongue testing the air, its rattles buzzing with an air of defiance.

Happy stood motionless, watching, until finally the snake uncoiled very slowly and began to move away. She was cautious, yet still curious, as the creature moved, and so she tagged along behind, following its

211

deliberate departure from the spot where it had lain basking in the sun.

Trailing along after the snake, Happy suddenly bounded ahead over some rocks and came to a stop in front of the snake. It immediately coiled and buzzed a new warning. Happy had come upon the snake too fast. She was too close. Just as she was turning away, it struck. Instinctively she jumped, but not before she felt the fangs tug at her side. Luxuriant as it was, her coat was not thick enough to protect her from the rattlesnake's bite. It recoiled and faced Happy again.

Immediately the bite began to tingle and burn, gradually becoming more painful. Happy was overwhelmed by a feeling of dislike for the bunched thing before her! Ready to do battle, she faced it and moved a step closer. It struck again, this time sinking its fangs into her face. Determined to conquer this annoying creature, Happy worried it with her paw and muzzle. Repeatedly, the snake struck at her in efforts to protect itself. The bites stung and burned. Happy slammed a huge paw down on the snake's body, and it struck again, this time on her front leg.

Happy's original game had now evolved into an intense need to protect herself. She grabbed the rattler in her big jaws; its muscular body writhed and struggled forcefully, wrapping itself around her muzzle. She shook her head to free herself from the coils, and the snake dropped to the ground. In a moment it collected itself again and coiled into a heap. The mass of patterned brown, gray and black did not move. Unblinking eyes stared ominously at its huge black adversary.

BLACK OAK

Despite its brave attempts at self-preservation, the grim mass of muscle and fangs was no match for the big dog. Suddenly, an overwhelming need to kill came over Happy. Again, she grabbed the snake in her mouth, shook it violently, then dropped it. White belly up, the big rattler twisted and writhed in the gravel and leaves. It made no more attempts to strike. The snake was dead. Happy pawed at it a few times, then turned and walked away.

The rattler's poison had begun to work. Happy felt its searing effects. She shook her head to rid herself of the growing discomfort, but the sensation did not go away. Her face and head burned as the poison spread through the system. Her foreleg hurt. As the strange feelings spread through her, Happy tried to hurry home, overwhelmed with a need for Will and the security she knew he would provide. The pain grew worse, and it became a struggle to keep moving.

It was dusk by the time Happy made it to the top of the clearing. Her body could go no further. Her side was swelling and so was her face, and the pain continued. Most of the venom had been deposited in her side with the first attack, but each area of damage was affected by the poison.

Will saw her come to the top of the clearing and lie down. He called to her and when she didn't get up, his heart suddenly felt cold. Fear gripped the pit of his stomach. Something was wrong with her. He ran up the hill to her. It seemed to him that it took forever to get to her side. His legs felt as though they were working in slow motion. His mind was racing with thoughts, but his body was in a molasses world where his muscles only gradually moved him in the direction of his precious companion. His heart pounded. He felt hot. Many fears crowded into his mind. He was afraid she had been shot. And he knew rattlers were an ever present danger.

Will's slow motion world dissolved quickly as soon as he reached Happy. She was panting rapidly and was obviously in pain. She tried to wag a greeting to him as he approached, which only deepened his fears that she was badly hurt. Pity welled up inside him. He knew that she had made a tremendous effort to get back to him.

He spoke softly to her, "Lady, Lady what's happened to you?" He knelt beside her. He wanted to put his hands over her all at once to ease her pain. In the half-light of evening, he could see no blood. But he could tell that her lips and face were puffy. He ran his hand down her side and back, checking for bleeding, and found the swelling on her left side. He examined the area with gentle fingers. Happy whined.

The dog gained strength from Will's presence and tried to get up. She was exhausted and dizzy. She crumpled to the ground with a groan and did not try again.

Will's first impulse was to carry her to the cabin. Then he thought about the fact that he really did not know what was wrong with her and he was afraid he might injure her more. "Easy, Lady," he comforted. "Easy. We'll get you fixed up as good as new." Then Will stood. "You rest there," he said. "I'll be back in a minute." He stroked her body with a gentle hand, then turned and hurried to the cabin.

215

When Will returned, he was carrying a blanket. He spread it on the ground and, as gently as possible, rolled Happy onto it. Speaking softly to her, he pulled the blanket along the ground. As he moved down the hill, Will chose the trail carefully to make it as easy on her as possible.

With Happy still cradled in the blanket, Will lifted her onto the porch, then dragged her into the cabin. By the time he got her inside it was nearly dark. Quickly and silently now, Will went to work. He lit a lantern and reached into his cabinet of home remedies for his bottle of arnica. He still wasn't sure what his Lady's problem was, but he knew she was in great pain. The arnica would act on the pain and maybe give her some relief.

Will brought the light down close enough to look for wounds. With his hands he folded back her thick coat to study the swelling on her side. It was not hard to see the wound that reddened the area. He was dreading what he knew he would find: two tiny holes in the middle of the wound—the mark of a rattlesnake!

Will felt sick in the pit of his stomach. He leaned back and set the lantern on the floor. Tears welled up in his eyes as he looked at his companion. He felt helpless and overcome with grief. "Am I going to lose her too?" he thought. He reached over and stroked the big dog gently from her head down to her tail. "Lady," he said softly, "Please live. Please live. Let me help you. Please don't die, don't . . . die!" Will's voice went hoarse with fear and anguish. He stopped speaking, and in the cabin there was no sound except for Happy's rapid breathing.

After the initial shock, Will's head cleared. He knew

what to do. He needed to keep her cool and quiet. He had to give her liquids and watch her carefully. She needed to know that he was there all the time, taking care of her and encouraging her to live and get well.

As Will sat by Happy in the soft light of the lantern, he recalled a clear vision of his boyhood. Occasionally, one of the family dogs had been bitten by a rattlesnake. He remembered watching his father care tenderly for the injured dog. And he remembered also that all but one of those dogs recovered.

Will had great respect for folk medicine. For years, he had practiced successful self-care. It wasn't that he didn't like doctors, but he'd learned that some things he could do for himself. He knew, also, that there were times when doctors were absolutely necessary. As he sat on the cabin floor with his hand on Happy's side, he made a great effort to recall what his father did so long ago to save the dogs.

"Cool towels," he said aloud. "Yes, lots of cool towels. Some on her head, some on her side. Change dressings over and over . . . change dressings." His words were hesitant at first as the thoughts formed. Then, as he became more sure of his direction, he spoke as though he was giving commands, voicing his plan aloud with assurance. "If she is willing, give her water. Dogs can live for days without food, but they must have water. And when she is able to take water, put some honey in it, then a bit of broth. And keep changing those towels." Hope filled him as he recalled the techniques of healing that he had learned as an observant boy. He hurried to his little medicine box and selected the right remedies

for swelling, inflammation, and pain; lachesis . . . cro-
talus . . . and arnica, always, arnica.

Will set to work in a frenzy. His Lady's life depended
on his ability to provide the proper care immediately.
He hurried to the pump for water. He pumped buckets
full, cool and fresh from the depths of the mountain,
and carried them to the cabin. He gathered towels and
rags, wet them in the water, and placed them over the
bites. Gently, he covered Happy's swollen muzzle and
head, leaving space so that she could breathe easily. He
covered her side with more towels. All the while he
spoke to the wounded dog, reassuring her that he would
stay with her.

When he finished covering her with towels, he
reached for his little bottle of arnica. As he shook the
bottle hard, acting out his determination, his childhood
rushed back to him once again. He could hear his
mother's voice saying, "Take this dear, it will help your
hurt to go away," as she eased some childhood mishap.
Will found himself now repeating those same words to
his wounded friend, as he lifted her big lip to drop a few
drops of the healing remedy into her mouth. The words
gave him confidence and comfort, just as they had so
long ago. Will smiled.

Happy was awake and aware of Will's presence and
care. Stoically, she accepted her pain. She opened her
eye, occasionally to watch Will, but she did not move.
Gradually, she relaxed and fell into a fitful sleep.

All through that first long night, Will tended to
Happy's needs. Over and over he removed the warmed

towels and applied cool ones, talking to her as he tirelessly cared for her poisoned body. He stroked her gently, hoping to ease her pain. His hands flowed over her
and then massaged each leg.

Suddenly, Happy yelped loudly and pulled her leg
away. Almost simultaneously, Will felt the hot and
swollen front leg. Another snakebite! Pity and anger
mingled as he assessed yet another insult to her body.
He wrapped the untended bite with cold cloths as he
apologized to her for causing her pain, chiding himself
for not being more thorough in the initial examination.
How could he have been so careless!

At daybreak, Will applied new coverings to all of
Happy's wounds, then sat back on the floor and looked
out the cabin's east window at the approaching dawn.
It surprised him to know he had worked with her all
night long. His knees felt sore and his hip joints were
tender when he moved. Reaching toward the dog, he
let his hand fall to rest on her side. He could feel the
pounding of her heart. She was still breathing rapidly.

"Good morning, Lady," he greeted her. "You've
made it through the night . . . that's good. Now, let's
make it through the day." Encouraged, Will gave her
another dose of healing remedy. He stroked her soft
neck with his big hand. At least for the moment, he felt
comforted. She was still alive! As he looked down at
her, he was suddenly overcome with a great weariness.

Will stretched out close to Happy and tried to doze,
but the hard floor and his tense muscles tortured him
too much to allow a peaceful sleep. His mind churned
with frustration and worry. Some of his dreams were

about his Lady; some were about old heartaches that lay buried deep in his memory.

The sun lifted above the mountains into a clear sky. As it rose, it pierced the dimly lit cabin and slowly tracked across the wooden floor, resting finally on the two sleeping forms. The warmth on Will's aching body helped his pains. He awakened and stretched his hand toward Happy. She was still, but he could feel her heart beat. He sat up, leaned over her and rested his ear on her chest. He could feel her rapid breathing and hear the pounding of her heart. "Beat heart, beat," he said softly, "I want her to live!"

For the next few days, Will watched steady improvement. By the morning of the fourth day, a gray and misty dawn, he was aware of a new strength about his dog. Her heart had ceased to pound so violently; it seemed more in unison with her easier breathing. Frequently, Happy moved her legs and lifted her head to look at Will. She drank a little of the broth he had made for her, and he took great comfort in her renewed interest in food.

The wounds on Happy's body were still very swollen. Each area was discolored and extremely sensitive to touch. In spite of her condition, however, she made attempts during the day to go outside. By evening, she was able to walk into the clearing. She walked a short distance, urinated, then headed for the water bucket at the pump. Will let her walk, following her with words of praise for her efforts. He was thrilled to see her moving. Her body tired before she reached her destination, and she sat down and turned her swollen face toward

Will. Her expression was easy to understand. Will responded quickly by delivering a pan full or freshly drawn water.

Happy lapped a few swallows, then rested, looking around the clearing. After a short time, Will helped her back to the cabin. He left the door open to let the evening's cooling breeze drift through the doorway. Contentment wafted over Happy. She stretched out full length on the cabin floor, breathed deeply and fell sound asleep. She was getting better.

Will had a good feeling about Lady as he closed up the cabin for the night. She watched him as he latched the door and stirred the embers of the little fire. He leaned over her and stroked her head. "Good night, pretty Lady," he chuckled to her. "This has been a better day for us, hasn't it?" Then Will crawled into bed for a peaceful sleep.

Late in the night, Happy's restlessness awakened Will. He lay in bed and listened to her moving about the cabin. She gave a low growl and a warning bark. Will had seldom heard her do that, and when she did it again, he felt sure there was an intruder in the clearing.

Quietly, Will got out of bed and slipped on his trousers, speaking softly to the dog as he did so. He opened the door to investigate and there was Wyn. As Will opened the door, she jumped off the porch and stood in the clearing. She was only a dim outline in the darkness, but he could see that her tail was waving gently. Will was sure she must have come for a meal, for whenever she came around, he always fed her.

Will found a match and lit the lantern. As he collected

some good things to eat, he realized that this other black dog had never been on the porch before. Had she come to see Lady? Will left the pan of food on the table and went to look out into the darkness again. Holding his light high, he ducked under the beam of light and greeted the big dog, "Hello Black. Maybe it's mostly your friend you came to see, huh? Well, that may be just what she needs." With that, Will stepped off the porch and walked out into the clearing. He sat down where he could be out of her way if she chose to go look for Lady.

Wyn watched him carefully. Usually when she came, the man fed her in the clearing, spoke a few words to her, and then she and Happy played a while before she left. She usually stayed around for a short time, then vanished into the forest. This time, the man's behavior was different. This puzzled her, and she watched him for a long time. At last she walked back to the porch, sat, then got up and paced back and forth, as though eagerly anticipating her meal.

Will sat patiently and silently. He wished for a pipe, but it was inside the cabin, and he did not want to disturb the restless dog.

When she continued to pace, he spoke to her, "Go ahead, Black; go see your friend. She's in there, Go find her." The word, find, triggered a behavior in Wyn's mind. It was a word from the past. It was a word her human used in play and training sessions. Wyn had heard it over and over again as a young dog. Now she responded. She knew it meant to search for something. Much to Will's surprise, she wagged her tail, put her nose down and began sniffing. Wyn really did not know what she was supposed to find, but the man's command urged her on. She hopped back up onto the porch, moved to the open doorway and stretched her neck into the darkened room.

Will waited expectantly. He was pleased that the dog was moving in Lady's direction. He saw her disappear through the cabin door. Will wished he could witness the scene unfolding inside his little home. But he realized he could not intrude. He was not needed. He heard the pan clatter to the floor . . . Black had found her dinner.

A few minutes later the big dog came back outside and hopped off the porch. She paused to look at Will, then moved past him in the lantern light and disappeared into the darkness.

Will got up, brushed the dirt from the seat of his trousers and went back into the cabin. Black had indeed found her dinner. The clean pan lay on the floor, pushed into a corner where she had wedged it as she ate.

He lowered the lantern to study Lady's reaction to the night visitor. To his delight, she sat up and looked at him with a bright expression, then turned her head toward the doorway. Expressing her pleasure, she gave a few wags of her tail.

Each evening after the first visit, Wyn returned to the clearing. For the next week, when Will saw her coming, he took his pipe and moved away from the cabin. Each evening, he sat intrigued by the routine they'd established. The black dog appeared and Will moved to his observation point, leaving her meal inside the cabin with

Happy. The visitor repeated her behaviors of the first
night, reappeared at the doorway, looked at Will and
then made her way back to her wild world.

By the end of the week, when Wyn appeared at the
doorway, Happy followed her outside. Wyn jumped off
the porch easily, and Happy stood quietly and watched
her leave.

Will knew that much of his Lady's healing could be
attributed to his own good care, but he also knew that
her spirits were boosted undeniably with each visit from
her companion. Again on this late September evening,
Will was reminded of how strongly those two were
bound. He admired the black dog that came to visit
Lady.

Will would never know Wyn's inner feelings. She
could not tell him of her human far away. She could not
explain about the pleasant hours they had spent together. She could not tell Will of the thrill of seeing a
human on horseback, the first human she had seen in
weeks, and of the fear and pain when the human turned
on her. If Will had known all of that, he could have
understood Wyn's scars. They ran deep in her, deeper
even than she realized. The day would come when all
of her past, her fears and joys would be put to another
difficult test.

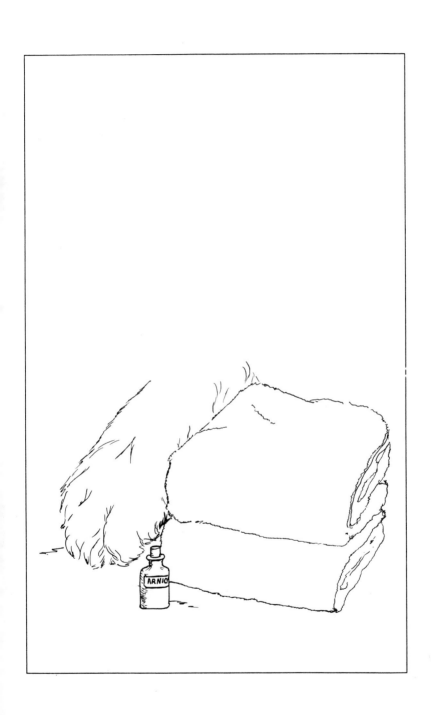

SEVENTEEN

LITTLE VISITORS

It was early October. When Will put Wyn's food down for her, it was already dark. "There you are, Black," he said. "You are a very good doctor. Our patient has healed well."

Will was accustomed to Wyn's appearance just before dark. She came to play, to socialize, and to eat. The ritual changed very little from evening to evening. As soon as she appeared, the dogs launched into vigorous play. When they had spent their energies, they flopped on the ground near the porch, both eying Will, waiting for their meal.

Ever since Wyn's first visit to Happy after the snakebite, she had become an important part of the healing process. Her presence offered a balm that Will could not provide. He tapped out his pipe on the porch post and went inside to light his lantern. It spread a warm glow over the room. He was just about to light the fire when

227

he heard a low growl in the clearing. He joined Happy on the porch, followed the direction of her gaze and realized the sound was coming from Wyn. He could see her shadowy presence in the darkness by her food dish. The growl came again, a soft warning.

Will retrieved the lantern from the cabin and moved off the porch toward Wyn. He moved cautiously, his eyes straining for clues in the low light. As he got closer, he could see that she was lying down with the pan of food held between her front paws, her head lowered over it protectively. Her attention was riveted ahead of her into the darkness so that she barely acknowledged Will's presence. She had eaten only a bite or two of her meal.

"Strange," he thought. "She is always such an eager eater."

He lifted the lantern higher and looked into the darkness for the cause of her behavior. Within moments, he saw a dark form emerging from the shadows. Slowly at first, then more quickly it moved toward Wyn. Suddenly, as if repelled by the lantern light, it backed away into the darkness. Will's arm ached from holding the lantern up, but he was afraid to move. It thrilled him to realize he had just seen one of Wyn's pups. Slowly, he backed away from the big dog and waited.

The pup appeared again. It moved towards its dam in a crouching position, lifting a curious muzzle to the new aroma of her meal. Again, she warned it with the same low growl. But the pup was determined. It darted toward the luscious fragrance. Quickly, Wyn snapped in the pup's direction, giving firm notice that she would not permit it to share this meal.

Will was fascinated by the scene unfolding before him. Gradually, he lowered the lantern, relieving his arm and shoulder, and at the same time providing better light close by where Black lay. Will looked intently into the darkness for more pups. He saw none.

"Surely she had more than one pup," he thought. "I wonder what happened to them?"

Another growl drew his attention back to the drama in the clearing. He watched with a growing respect for the pup's determination and the mother's controlled attitude as she continued to deny food to her pup. Deliberately, Wyn took a bite of her meal, all the while watching warily for any move the pup might make. She continued this behavior until the youngster no longer attempted to come near her food. Content that the pup had learned its lesson, Wyn cleaned up the last crumbs, stood and shook. With a parting glance at Will, she turned and disappeared into the forest.

The bewildered pup watched her leave, then scampered over to investigate the empty pan. It licked and licked to salvage any remaining vestige of the meal. Will watched motionless as the pup satisfied its curiosity. Suddenly, the young canine became acutely aware of the man's presence. It lifted its head and stared at him, evaluating a new experience. Standing face-to-face with the first human it had ever seen or smelled, the pup wrestled with conflicting instincts—curiosity and caution. Slowly, wild heritage overpowered concentration, and the pup backed a few steps away. After one final glance at Will, it started up the slope toward its mother. At the edge of the clearing, a smaller pup darted out with

229

a wriggling greeting, and together the pair bounded off into the darkness. But the curious pup carried with him a clear vision of the unmoving figure illuminated by lantern light. He remembered the scent of man. He remembered the scent of the meal he never shared, and he felt no fear of what he had seen and smelled.

As far as Will knew, this was the first time Wyn had brought her young with her to the cabin. To them, it was just another exciting adventure, another learning experience. But to Will, it was a memorable event. He had longed to see Wyn's pups. He was sure they were offspring of a coyote mating, and he had spent sometime designing in his mind what he thought they would look like. Now he knew, and he knew there were at least two of them.

The pups were five months old. Their needle sharp baby teeth had been replaced by adult teeth, large and gleaming white. Wyn's milk supply had dwindled, and the youngsters now shared in the kills made by their parents. They were old enough to go along on long hunts, experiences that offered constant challenges.

As the autumn days passed, Wyn occasionally came to the cabin earlier in the day. Will made it a habit to check the area carefully when she appeared. He always had food ready for her, and he hoped to toss a few bits to the young ones that traveled with her. He couldn't count on Happy to announce their presence. They were her friends; she merely accepted their appearance as routine. In fact, Happy found the youngsters to be pleasant company now. They were amusing and enjoyable. She spent a great deal of time playing games with them.

MOUNTAIN MAHOGANY

After a few encounters, Will felt satisfied that there were only two pups. In size, build and behavior, the little one looked so much like her father that Will was amazed. Only the pups' identical color assured him they were of the same mating. Most of their puppy fuzz was gone now, except atop their heads and around their large ears. They were dressed in shining coats of black-tipped hair over a soft tan and gray underlining. Black legs and tan feet hinted of the pups' coyote ancestry. The male's broad head and folded ears looked much like his dam's. But the little female's ears flopped over just slightly at the tips, a strong reminder of her sire.

In personality, also, the young female imitated her wild and wary coyote sire. She was hesitant and skittish near the cabin. Any brashness she may have felt in her natural surroundings dissolved completely when she caught sight of Will. She took no comfort in her mother's acceptance of the human. To the young pup, Will was a strange new animal, large and frightening, and definitely not to be trusted. Day after day, as the little family returned to the clearing, she remained curious, but aloof, venturing only occasionally from the underbrush at the edge of the slope.

By contrast, the male pup gradually became relaxed enough to follow Wyn halfway into the clearing. He established an imaginary barrier beyond which he would not go. From this vantage point, in plain sight of the human, he listened and learned as his mother spent time with Happy and Will.

Will enjoyed the puppy's interest in the big dogs' activity. Occasionally, caught up in the excitement, the pup would wag his tail and make short leaping hops in their direction. When the dogs ran near him in their games of chase, he ran short distances with them, but he was always careful not to cross his imaginary line.

Each time Wyn and the pups came to the clearing, Will tried to remain the silent observer. He was always willing to take time from his workshop to watch the dogs play out their energies. He was extremely careful not to frighten the big pup when it was in the clearing. It showed great curiosity.

Meal time seemed a good opportunity to establish a friendship. As he emerged from the cabin with the dogs' food, he called Wyn and Happy. Although he never looked directly at him, he was aware the pup was watching him. The hungry dogs galloped toward him, eager for their dinners. With a meal in each hand, Will walked out into the clearing a few steps and put a pan down for Happy. Using Wyn as his decoy, he moved slightly in the direction of the pup.

"Here, Black," he said softly as he put her food down. "How 'bout some good biscuits and meat for your dinner?" He waved the pan above her.

The pup watched his mother's tail wagging playfully as her head moved in perfect unison with the dinner pan. From a discrete distance, he caught a whiff of the food and lifted his muzzle to sniff. Will watched him as he set the dinner on the ground for Wyn. He took an extra biscuit from the pan and tossed it toward the puppy, a safe distance from Wyn. The youngster flinched, but did not run.

"Here, fella," Will offered, "How about a taste of

bread for you?" The young male cocked his head at the sound of the human voice.

Will retreated to the porch and sat down. The pup eyed him curiously, then moved toward the biscuit. He sniffed it, cautiously at first, then with great interest. He licked it and touched it with his paw. Still watching Will, the youngster picked up the biscuit, ran a few feet toward the forest, and then stopped long enough to wolf it down.

All the while, the wild and worried female was hiding in the shadowy edges of the forest, afraid to come near the human. She watched her brother as he came up the slope toward her, but before she could attack him, he had devoured his prize. She was never able to overcome the instincts that kept her distant and fearful.

In contrast, the male pup found the clearing a fascinating place. He felt no fear of the human, but he did remain cautious. He saw Happy on Will's porch and watched the two together. He watched his mother eagerly accept food from the human, and soon he, too, came to enjoy the handouts from Will's kitchen.

GOOD-BY. . .

The chill nights vitalized the mountain creatures. It affected Wyn and her mate as well. Night after night, the coyote sat alert, straining to hear the voices of his own kind drifting to his ears. The many voice tones he heard obviously came from a family group. The young, inexperienced ones chimed in with the deeper, more practiced adults. Yipping and yapping, the youngsters tried in vain to mimic the tribe elders, but their juvenile voices were no match. Still, they expressed their excitement at being alive and free.

The full moon bathed Wyn and her mate in its reflected light. Responding to the distant calls, the coyote sounded three short yaps, then waited. Wyn came to sit beside him and listen. As the distant choir warbled and then quieted again, the big coyote replied with his own lyrics. Then, as if on cue, Wyn raised her own deep voice to join the wild song. Excited, the pups joined

237

their parents, and suddenly all four were singing in the moonlit night. They responded twice to the distant group. Then, as quickly as it all began, the singing stopped, and silence returned to the mountain. After a time, the pups relaxed, stretched out and slept.

But a sense of excitement lingering in the air stimulated Wyn and her mate. Alert and curious, the coyote stood and sniffed for signals of the pack. Nothing. He moved away from the ledge and up to the ridge above, and sniffed again. Still, nothing. Restless, he paced along the vantage point above their home. Back and forth, back and forth. At last, he turned in the direction of the now silent voices and disappeared. When Wyn could no longer hear him, she jumped up and bounded after him, determined that he would not travel this night alone.

The moon dropped behind the hills, and the new day dawned. As the sun came up, it cast streams of light across the sleeping pups. They began to stretch and change positions as their bodies warmed. Bird calls penetrated their sound sleep. Finally, a buzzing insect caused the male to sit up and shake his head. He looked over at his sister. His tail wagged with anticipation. Crouching low, he pounced. Her eyes opened just in time to see the attack coming. At once, she was awake, and they were at play, tumbling and wrestling, working themselves farther and farther from the ledge.

The ledge had continued to serve as headquarters for most of the family's activities. Wyn and the coyote had spent much time teaching the young ones to hunt for themselves. Sometimes, the family hunted in pairs. Occasionally, all four hunted together.

CALIFORNIA SISTER BUTTERFLY

Both pups had a deep instinct to chase, and they were quick to pick up the hunting skills of their parents. Their dexterity was improving. Often, they managed to catch mice, frogs or gophers. And one of their greatest joys was digging for ground squirrels.

Along with their hunting skills, the pups developed more and more independence. The two had begun wandering on short, unchaperoned journeys away from the ledge. Urged on by her persistent curiosity, the female led the way on frequent jaunts. She felt driven by a never-ending desire to learn more about her world.

Today, as their youthful energies abated, thirst led the pups to a favored drinking pool. Then hunger prompted them toward more serious duties. For an hour or more, they worked to locate a few morsels of food . . . a mouse here, some berries there, a few beetles and grubs underneath a shrub or a log. Tirelessly, the little female led the tour.

At last, the big male stopped. He had gone as far as he cared to go on this morning's journey. He sat and watched as his sister disappeared down the path, leaping and pawing the air in pursuit of a butterfly. It didn't seem to matter to her whether he followed or not. Nature had given her a mandate to travel.

Since infancy, independence had been her strength. Now she was armed with basic survival skills. She approached each new experience fearlessly. She looked back only once . . . long enough to see her brother scampering back down the trail toward home.

A brown bird scratching under a bush caught her attention. It flew ahead of her, just out of reach. She leaped and missed, then watched it fly. Head lifted and tail, wagging, she seemed undaunted by failure. Life was a game beckoning to her young spirit. She dashed off to meet its adventures head on.

The young male quickly widened the distance between them. He saw no more joy in the hunt and wanted to go home. Sniffing his earlier trail along the way, he responded to an instinct to retrace his steps back to the ledge. He galloped, then walked, then galloped again, occasionally checking for scent. The thoughts of his safe den tugged at him as he hurried home alone.

When Wyn and the coyote returned from their moonlit journey, both pups were gone. Wyn searched the outer area, thoroughly studying the scents she found there. She looked about her, then moved around the path to the ledge. She examined it also and concluded her pups were nowhere around. She woofed once, expecting to call them back. Then a bit of movement in the distance caught her eye. Alert, she stiffened and watched intently. Whatever it was, it was heading straight for her. It came closer, then suddenly began moving faster. At that moment, Wyn realized it was her male pup.

Seeing his parents, spurred on by the joy of success, the young male expended all of his energies. When he reached his parents at last, he gleefully wiggled and jumped at them, biting and nipping to express his great relief and pleasure at their presence. Then he settled down to rest, savoring the security of familiar surroundings.

The little female never returned. Her parents had given her all they could . . . health, intelligence and

241

ability. She would meet life's challenges and succeed because she had learned her lessons well. As with the little whelp that died at birth, there would be no sadness, no mourning, no grieving. With the animal world's calm acceptance, her family would not question her absence. By her choice, her life with them was over. With ease, they let her go.

BUILDING TRUST

It was dawn. Happy awakened and lifted her head. The frosty October night painted her in crystalline art. As she slept, her warm breath streamed out into the night air and drifted about her face. It was transformed into minute frozen particles that had gathered on her black coat. Her ears and the top of her head were lightly dusted with a powdered sugarcoating. The frost gathered heavily on her eyebrows and the whiskers on her muzzle were covered with delicate icy crystals. She looked like an ancient matriarch, silvered by age.

A movement by the chicken house caught Happy's attention. It was Wyn, standing guard once again in her old spot. By her side sat the young male pup. The youngster and his dam had hunted with the coyote part of the night. The trail back to their den led past Will's cabin. This was where she wanted to be. The pup followed her and, reluctantly, so had the coyote.

Many times in the past, the coyote had tried to lure Wyn from the clearing. But if she wasn't ready to go, there was nothing he could do but accept her behavior. He paced restlessly. This was not a place where he could ever feel comfortable. He remembered the chase after he had stolen Will's old rooster, and remembering stirred fear deep within him. Eventually, his instincts drove him to move on. Not far away, he heard a familiar coyote chorus. With a vague feeling of discontent, he loped off. He had no real desire to return to the ledge, and he was lured by the calls from his own kind. Nudged by his loneliness, he turned in the direction of their voices.

★ ★ ★ ★ ★

The squeak of the big hinges turned Happy's attention to the heavy cabin door. It swung open, and there stood Will. "Good morning, Lady," he said, ruffling the soft coat behind her ears with both hands. Welcoming his attention, Happy responded with a resonant woof. She was stimulated by the cold morning, and she leaped off the porch, circled the clearing at a run and bounced back up onto the porch to Will.

Wyn watched from the top of the slope. Her tail waving gently. She longed to be a part of Will's and Happy's play. Finally, she could resist no longer and galloped down the slope to join the fun. Deliberately she stole Happy's attention from Will, and led her friend òff to play in the clearing.

Will was content to stand back and watch the two. He was never surprised to see Black anymore. She came frequently and unexpectedly, as she had since Happy's snakebite.

As Will turned to go back inside, he saw the young pup come slowly but confidently down the slope and into the clearing. The pup's attention was riveted on the adult dogs at play. Step by step, he drew nearer to the rowdy pair. He crouched low, ready to pounce, as the adults tumbled past. They ignored him. Finally, at an opportune moment he threw himself into their games. Still, the older dogs continued playing as though he had never appeared. He was satisfied just to be a part of the fun. He nipped and grabbed, pushed and pounced with the adult dogs until all three grew tired of the play and flopped down to rest.

It was time for breakfast. Three sets of eyes turned toward Will expectantly. He headed for his kitchen. Three mouths to feed. His family was growing! He had to cut the rations a bit, because he hadn't expected a third guest. But it pleased him to fix a pan of food for the young one. Yes, the more he thought about it, the better he liked the idea.

The big dogs were eager for their meal. Will went through the usual ceremony. Each had a special place for her pan, and each was willing to wait her turn. He fed the two females, then turned to the pup who stood watching the older ones devouring their food, his tail wagging with anticipation. Will moved toward the pup, talking softly and holding out a small bit of food. The pup showed little fear, but not wanting to push his luck, Will set the pan down and returned to the porch so the pup could eat undisturbed.

The youngster remembered the fresh biscuit Will had tossed him a few days ago. Here was that good fragrance again. He sauntered over to the pan and sniffed it carefully. It also carried the strong scent of man, yet that did not worry him. He longed to eat. Will saw Black make a move toward the pup and called her name. She looked at him, fully understanding, then moved away, letting the pup finish his breakfast undisturbed.

Will watched the puppy closely. He could see now that it was a male. He admired the strong legs and sturdy body, so like his mother's. He liked the big ears that flopped over the sides of the pup's broad head. He wondered if they would ever stand up fully like coyote ears. Will found the pup's expression especially pleasing. He seemed trusting. There was a casual air about him, in spite of his youth.

Will was acutely aware that Wyn and her pup were spending more time around the place. Occasionally, he tried to make friends with the growing youngster. But the pup kept his distance, perhaps because his mother did. When Happy was around, he was able to lure the pup closer. Once it followed Happy up on the porch, close enough for Will to touch, but his common sense told him not to reach out. The curious pup stretched forward to investigate Will's boots and trousers, then hopped off the porch and sat watching as Will stroked Happy and talked to her softly.

Will knew the pup was learning, and he took great pleasure in these moments. "I'd sure like to have you for a friend," Will said to the watchful youngster. "It would be great to have another fellow around the place."

★ ★ ★ ★ ★

Autumn had dried the mountain grasses and colored the leaves. There was occasional rain, a hint of the rainy season that was soon to come to the back country—all part of nature's continuing pattern of change.

Wyn's attitude was changing, too. It had nothing to do with the season or the weather, but deeply buried feelings were making their way to the surface. She would have turned for home long ago, but the rancher's rifle had delayed her. She would have tried again in the late spring, but motherhood gave her another purpose for living. Now, for a third time, Wyn's internal drives were calling her home.

Once again her coyote mate faced the difficulty of dealing with her domestic behaviors. Wyn had almost completely forsaken him as her mate. The female pup's disappearance had been a catalyst for her inner restlessness. Not long after that, she'd taken up residence again at the clearing, reclaiming her place as a distant member of Will's family.

The coyote came for her many times, cajoling and demanding that she rejoin him in his wild style, but his efforts were ineffective.

Wyn felt a longing that would not let her return to life with the coyote. She was irritable at times. She was impatient with the puppy and short-tempered with Happy.

Will watched and listened. He had seen this behavior in the Black before. He knew she was about to make a move. He wondered whether Lady would leave with

OF HERITAGE AND HEART

her friend or stay with him. For many days now, Will had smoked his pipe without seeing the smoke plumes. His feelings and thoughts were turned inward. Finally, he made a decision that would affect them all.

The bond between Lady and Black Dog was one of the closest Will had ever seen in the animal world or even in the world of humans. Over the past months, he witnessed incredible examples of the deep need the two dogs had for one another. He admired and envied these two friends for what they shared, and he knew the greatest gift he could give them would be to accept their decisions.

"If Black leaves . . . ," he whispered to himself. "When Black leaves . . . if Lady needs to go with her, she must go." Tears welled in his eyes as he realized the consequences of his vow. It hurt him to think how empty the clearing would be without the three dogs, but especially without Lady. Will was a strong man who honored his convictions, but as he imagined the loneliness he knew would come, his pain overflowed and tears streamed silently down his weathered face into his beard.

Will cast a sweeping glance around his home. He had become so accustomed to seeing the dogs sprawled out in the sun, or curled under a shady shrub. They were good company. It was a part of everyday life for him to know they were nearby. His eyes moved to the sleeping pup, and his anxiety eased. Perhaps . . . just perhaps, he could arrange for the pup to stay with him after Black left. He had no way of controlling Lady, but he was sure he could control the little one that lay sleeping so innocently. Yes. Yes! He would keep the pup!

He was sure he could tame him. He was already working on that. The pup was learning to trust him. Day by day, the youngster had become more relaxed around him. It would be only a matter of time until he felt entirely comfortable with Will. Gradually, Will began to formulate a plan for the capture. He looked around the clearing for the best place to build a small pen. A high fence, he thought, that ought to hold him. Maybe he should add boards along the bottom so he couldn't dig out. Will realized he was going against all he'd ever believed about confining an animal; he had never liked to see a dog penned or tied. It seemed so unnatural and terribly unfair to the animal. But, he could think of no other way to keep the pup from leaving. "Just for a while," he promised the sleeping puppy, "just until we become friends. Then you may have your freedom."

Will planned the capture carefully. He didn't want to frighten the pup, but he wanted him safely restrained so that when the Black finally decided to leave, he wouldn't follow.

Will gathered tools, posts and wire fencing, and began building the pen. He worked feverishly, driven by his nagging certainty of the Black's inevitable departure, and perhaps Lady's, too. As he watched the pen take shape, the final plan came clear in his mind.

Once the pen was finished, he would leave the gate open and feed all three dogs inside. Yes, that would work! They would come and go as they wished. Surely neither of the big dogs would mind. They trusted him. Even the pup was distantly friendly. Once the dogs were used to eating their meals in the pen, it would be no problem to separate the pup from the adults. Will stood back and looked at the result of two days of effort. He was pleased. The pen was solid and secure. The gate was tight to the ground. Will put his tools away. He was ready for the next step in his plan.

Three hungry friends greeted him as he carried their suppers out of the cabin that evening. Will led the way through the gate, and the adults rushed in behind him, eager to eat. He set the three pans down in separate corners of the pen and left.

The puppy refused to enter the gate with the older dogs. Smelling the food, he darted up and down the outside of the fencing. Wyn finished her own meal and turned to the pup's pan of food.

Will stepped back in and picked it up. "Now, Black," he scolded softly, "don't you think you've had enough?" After a while, both dogs seemed satisfied there was no more food in the pan, and they wandered out for a drink at the pump and an after-dinner nap.

Will watched the hungry pup explore the outer edges of the pen. He was still looking for his meal. Will carried the pup's pan back into the enclosure. He set it down just a few feet inside the gate, then retreated to the porch to watch. He had barely gotten out of the way when the eager pup rushed up to the gate. Stretching his neck toward the food, he sniffed and looked just once behind him, as if to see if anyone was watching. Cautiously, he moved into the pen and cleaned his plate.

During the next few days, Will watched his plan in action. The dogs seemed comfortable with the new routine. Gradually, the pup accepted his meals in the pen as easily as the adults did. As he watched the dogs, Will fully accepted what he knew was to come. He even allowed himself to admit that Lady would leave, too. But he concentrated now on making friends with the young male, and each day he made progress. He owed a great deal of his success to Happy's trusting nature. Her example made it easier for the pup to accept Will without fear.

Then Will began closing the gate . . . just during the time the dogs ate their meals. Then he would open it and set them free. Occasionally, he would feed Lady and the pup at the same time, even if Wyn was not around. His plan was going well.

"Next," he thought, "I will feed the pup alone in the fenced area . . . and close the gate . . . just long enough for him to eat. Then I will set him free." As he carried the three breakfast pans outside, the young male came loping toward him from his post at the top of the clearing. Lady and the Black were nowhere in sight. Keeping his eyes on the food, the pup hopped eagerly around Will as he moved into the enclosure. Speaking softly, he set one pan of food on the ground. Still, the two adult dogs had not arrived. So, Will walked out of the enclosure and closed the gate. For a long time, he sat on the porch with the two pans of food beside him, waiting for the two dogs to come bounding out of the forest. But they never came.

RESCUE

Happy trotted willingly along with Wyn. What she had at first accepted as a short hunt had now lengthened into a day away from Will and their home in the clearing. She trailed along with no thought of a farewell to the kind man on the mountain. Happy was keenly aware of the intensity of this mission. Although she had thoughts of turning back, something in Wyn's attitude convinced her to continue.

Wyn moved with purpose. She hunted only to appease her hunger. She rested only for short periods. The longer she traveled, the more intense her feelings became. Once again, after many months' delay, she was caught up in this single-minded effort of finding her home.

The Santa Ana winds blew warm across the mountains. Dry air flowed in from the desert, and drove fiercely through the passes toward the ocean. In the valleys, the temperature rose far above normal for the season.

The Newfoundlands were still many miles from their home near the sea. With only instinct to guide her, Wyn hunted in earnest for any clues that would help lead her home. She carried with her a deep need to feel her human's hands and hear her human's voice. She wanted desperately to be with the woman she remembered. And she pursued her quest relentlessly.

The parched Santa Ana air and burning sun made travel difficult during the day, so Wyn and Happy spent the late morning and early afternoon resting in whatever shade they could find. But even then, Wyn's senses did not rest. Which way must she go? Where was home . . . her home? And where was her human?

It was easy to follow the mountain trails. There were firebreaks to travel and paths made by animals on the way to water. As the sun lowered in the sky, Wyn jumped to her feet. It was time to go.

They had already come a great distance from Will's cabin. New territory meant they must search for water. Wyn sniffed the air for the smell of moisture. A slight hint sent her to investigate. Happy, too, caught scent of water, and together they followed the clues. As the scent grew stronger, they picked up speed. At last, they came to a small trickle seeping from under a ledge. They dug away at the saturated soil and allowed the basin to fill, then satisfied their thirst before moving on.

Sometime after dark, Wyn suddenly stopped and raised her head. She'd heard something, something familiar. The sound came again, and she identified it. It was laughter, lilting and happy, a woman's laughter. Both dogs were drawn toward the sound. They headed in its direction as fast as they could travel through unknown territory, picking their way over rocks and down a steep slope. Soon, they saw a campfire through the trees and, as they came closer, a young couple was sitting by the fire.

The woman's voice was the first female voice the dogs had heard since they'd left their kennel home nearly eleven months ago. Side by side, Happy and Wyn edged into the light of the campfire and then stopped, heads up and tails wagging. Wyn was hardly aware of the man. She focused her attention entirely on the young woman.

From that point on, it seemed that everything happened in a single moment. The woman caught a glimpse of the two dogs in the firelight and screamed. "Bears! Oh my God, bears!" Her voice trailed off into uncontrollable wailing. Drawn by the young woman's distress, Wyn headed toward her. But the man came to his companion's rescue, raving at the two dogs to get back and pounding on them with his hiking stick. Almost immediately, he had realized they were dogs and not bears, but he could not reassure his hysterical friend.

Feeling the intensity of the man's anger and frustration, Wyn turned and fled into the security of the forest, with Happy at her heels. As quickly as the melee had begun, it was over. But again the fear of man had clutched at Wyn. For her, the arduous miles of travel were focused on finding a special human; a woman with a soft voice and kind hands.

The backpackers sat for a time in stunned silence. Even the sounds of the crackling brush quieted as the dogs ran for safety from the scuffle. The young woman's fears slowly subsided. The two young people were left groping in the darkness for their cooking equipment as well as their composure. It was a terribly frightening moment to them, and in the morning they would wonder briefly if it really had happened. The huge paw prints in the soft earth would be there as proof.

It was dawn before Wyn stopped again. She and Happy had traveled a long way from the backpackers and Wyn's anxiety had eased. The two dogs walked a trail that threaded along the top of a ridge, then wound down a long gradual slope. Wyn sniffed the air, sensing the sweet smell of water. She kept moving, motivated now by thirst.

Happy trotted out ahead of her companion. Her nose told her that water was very near. The trail opened onto a grassy meadow that spread before them like a soft brown carpet. Happy was first to see the lake. She burst into a gallop, with Wyn close behind. Both of the dogs loved the water. After their scare at the campfire and an all-night journey, nothing could give them more pleasure now than cool, fresh water.

Happy stopped at the water's edge just long enough to sniff, then waded in belly-deep, drinking as she went. Wyn first drank closer to shore, then joined her companion further out. Ripples spread over the surface of the lake around the two dogs. Overhead, a stellar jay squawked his alarm at their early morning intrusion. As Wyn and Happy moved farther from shore, a fish darted

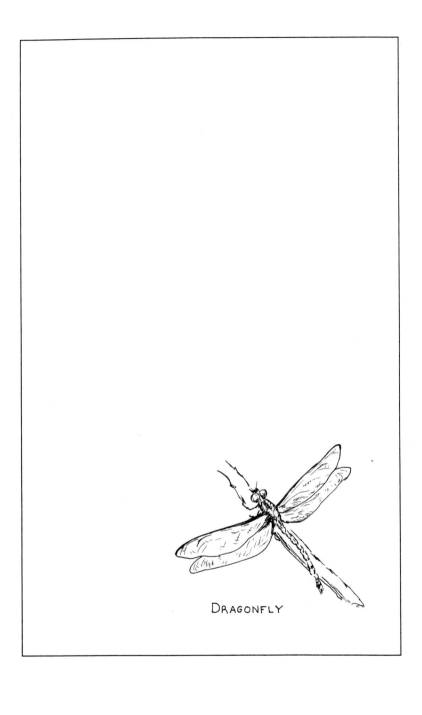

DRAGONFLY

away in the crystal water. This was the first deep water either of them had seen since they'd left their home near the Pacific coast, their first freshwater swim since they'd left their home in the Midwest. It was both comforting and refreshing.

A dragonfly darted by on invisible wings. Wyn followed it as it flitted erratically above the water. Soon her curiosity waned, and she swam back to Happy. After about half an hour, satisfied with their swim, the two dogs waded ashore. They shook violently to shed their heavy load of water. Then Wyn took the lead as they began investigating the shoreline. When she came to a rocky ledge along one side of the lake, Wyn climbed up to its flat stone surface and stretched out in the shade of a low shrub.

Happy nosed along the small beach searching for frogs in the wet grass. When one leaped just ahead of her, she pounced and missed. She took only a step or two toward it before its long, powerful legs thrust it to safety underwater. Tiring of the game and suddenly overcome with weariness, Happy followed Wyn's trail away from the water and up onto the secluded ledge.

For the second day, the Santa Ana winds gusted relentlessly through the mountains. Here on the ledge in the shade, the weary travelers could relax. Their night's journey had been a hard one. Now, after their refreshing swim, they could take refuge here.

Wyn looked down over the lake. She needed the rest. She settled her head comfortably between her outstretched paws, and drew in the first breath of a restful sleep.

The gusty wind blew their coats dry as both New-foundlands slept.

★ ★ ★ ★ ★

Mike Mortell climbed the ridge from the west. His map indicated the lake should be over the next rise past the bald summit. When the peak appeared above the ridge, he smiled. Mike loved maps. He was always grateful to those who had charted the trails before him. His destination today was Emerald Lake. He was almost there.

The sweatband around his forehead was saturated. It was an incredibly warm day for this time of year. Mike planned to set up camp at the little lake marked on his map. He hoped fervently that he would be the only one there for he enjoyed the feeling of being alone. Time to sense the wilderness—not tainted by human sounds and human presence. He had met only one other person so far, a man familiar with the territory who assured him that few day-hikers attempted this area's arduous trails. Mike kept thinking of the lake. If he had calculated the map correctly, he should be there by noon.

It was Mike's custom to hike for fifty minutes, then rest for ten. In the rising heat, ten minutes no longer seemed enough, but he decided to push on over the final ridge between himself and the lake. Mike developed a rhythm as he walked. He knew he was making good time. His whole being smoldered with satisfaction as he experienced the sounds and aromas of the wilderness. But it was getting hotter. Mike's breathing became la-bored, and his thigh muscles ached as he tackled the last steep grade to the top of the ridge and crested the summit. He was nearly exhausted.

Mike stopped for another brief rest under the shade of a huge evergreen. He was both surprised and frustrated to be so out of condition. The week before, he'd had a bout with the flu, but he hadn't expected it to affect his stamina profoundly. His pack was not heavy. He carried only a four-day supply of food and a canteen. He shouldn't be so tired. He decided his problem must be the hot dry winds combined with his recent illness.

A narrow trail threaded its way along the ridge line ahead of him, just as his map indicated. Mike smiled again, reached into his pack and pulled out a plastic bag of peanut butter balls, his favorite hiking treat. He ate each one slowly, savoring the rich, sweet reward.

From his position on the ridge, Mike could see a great distance to the north. The surrounding mountains seemed close enough to touch. The air was clear and sweet, bathed with the distinctive fragrance of evergreens warmed by the sun. He felt better now. Mike reached for his canteen and took a few swallows of water, then hooked it again to his pack. He studied the trail ahead. If his calculations were correct, the lake was just over a low rise at the base of craggy rocks he could see in the distance. He moved on, eagerly, his heart pounding.

Just as he expected, the lake came into view as he crested the rise. With each step, he could see more and more of its shimmering face. The lake was bordered on two sides by steep cliffs. It would be hard to get down to the beach. Mike sat down to take in the view. It was all he expected it to be and more: a pristine jewel, bathed in the mid-day sun, glistening and rippling under the hot Santa Ana winds that swooped down and blasted the surface. The water was crystal clear, deep and inviting. How beautiful! Mike wished he had provisions enough to stay longer. He scanned the shore and the surrounding area. He was grateful that no one else was in sight.

By the time Mike had worked his way down the north side of the lake shore, another hour had gone by. He was in no hurry, but with his pack, the descent was difficult. Each step he took drew him closer to the lake. Its beauty teased him as he caught glimpses through trees and shrubs. At last, the trail widened and opened onto a broad clearing that ran along the whole eastern edge of the lake. Mike walked across the grassy slope and stopped to peer into the clear waters. Slipping out of his pack, he flexed and stretched. He kneeled at the water's edge and met his likeness . . . tousled blond hair and a lean well-featured face, dripping with perspiration. The image fragmented and disappeared as he dipped his hands into the water for a satisfying drink.

Mike stood. Looking out across the lake, he felt like an explorer discovering a new continent. He reached up and pumped his arms in exhilaration. Then his attention turned to setting up camp. He selected a spot a short distance from the lake shore and pitched his tent. Its bright orange fabric fluttered gently in the wind against a vibrant backdrop of lingering fall colors and evergreens. Mike stood back and surveyed his campsite. It looked as perfect as a calendar picture.

The winds ruffled mirrored reflections on the water's surface. Rocky cliffs dressed in occasional greenery disintegrated into smatterings of color. As he watched the rippling water, Mike felt drawn toward it, as if by an inexplicable force. He stripped to his cut-offs and stepped in. It was colder than he expected. He splashed himself with a few hands full of water to adjust to its chill, shivering as he did so. Sharp rocks on the lake bottom convinced him it was easier to swim than wade. Although not an accomplished swimmer, Mike felt comfortable with his abilities. He leaned forward, stretching his arms ahead of him and pushed off forcefully.

On the ledge above the lake, the splash roused Wyn from her sleep. She lifted her head, waiting. Movement in the water soon had her focused on the figure swimming below. She could see his every stroke in the clear water. Farther and farther he swam toward the center of the lake.

Mike felt drawn by an urgency to be totally a part of this natural world. The opposite shore beckoned to him . . . challenging . . . inviting. He pushed on, enjoying the experience completely. The cold water rippled around his body. He felt primitive and strong. But soon he began to tire. His strokes became awkward, losing the reach and strength to carry him gracefully. His body splashed from side to side with each stroke.

Still watching from her ledge hideaway, Wyn quivered now as the splashing sounds began to unleash innate feelings. She tensed.

Feeling his fatigue, Mike looked around for the closest

shoreline and headed for in that direction. He was tired and much too cold. His breathing became more and more difficult. He was near panic, but he knew he needed all of his energy to reach the shore. It seemed so far away. He tried to compose himself, to collect his feelings and channel his energies toward reaching the shore. The cold penetrated deeper, numbing his body. His arms felt too heavy to lift. Suddenly, he realized his bad judgement might well cost him his life. The shore was just too far away. Instinctively, he cried out for help.

The sound drove Wyn to action. She bolted from the ledge and dashed down the slope to the shore nearest to the swimmer. Leaping into the water, she made two lunging jumps in his direction, and the lake bottom fell away beneath her. She swam at full speed toward the human. Her strong muscles and webbed feet propelled her so powerfully that the water surged and boiled behind her shoulders. Her head was lifted high out of the water and her brown eyes were fastened on the drowning man. With each breath, she expressed her distress in an agonizing sound, part whine, part growl.

It was a sound that was part of her heritage. It signaled the Newfoundland dog at perfection, striving to save a life. Wyn moved as though one with her ancestors. She had no thoughts now of the man who had wounded her. She felt no hesitation to help this stranger. Both heritage and heart united to compel her to his rescue. She must respond! She must get to him! She could feel his need and his distress as she closed the distance between them.

Mike saw the animal coming toward him in the water,

and his fear intensified. His numb body no longer responded, but he could feel the determination in those brown eyes that were fixed on him. He felt helpless, and wanted to escape, but he was unable to do so. As Wyn reached him he tried to turn away, but the big dog kept circling him and making strange noises. With his last bit of energy, Mike pushed the animal away in a futile attempt to protect himself.

Wyn was competent and knew her job well. Yet, in all her water rescue training, she had never encountered a problem like this. The human was supposed to hold onto her so she could tow him to shore. She had come to him, knowing he needed help, and he had pushed her away. Whining in frustration, she made another pass around the man, then clamped her jaws around his upper arm and turned toward shore.

Mike felt himself moving through the water, but he wasn't sinking. He felt pain where the animal's mouth gripped his arm, but the teeth were not tearing at him. Even though his mind was nearly numb with fear, he realized that the animal was dragging him through the water. Feeling a sudden surge of hope, he reached up and grabbed the animal's fur. He became aware of the rhythmic pattern of each stroke, the animal's breathing, and its strange crying sounds as it powered him toward shore. "I'm going to make it," he thought. "By some miracle, I'm not going to drown!"

When Wyn reached wading depth, she released her hold on Mike's arm. His hand still clutched her tightly, and she dragged him a few more feet, until his head and shoulders cleared the water, before he released his grasp on her heavy coat. She stood over him, dripping water on his face. Mike opened his eyes and looked up at her. He felt the ground and the rocks beneath him. He was acutely aware of her brown eyes looking down at him.

Wyn nudged him with her nose and sniffed around his face and upper body, particularly the arm damaged by her teeth. It was bleeding. With great effort, Mike pulled himself out of the cold water and onto the bank. He could feel the animal snuffling his head. He opened his eyes again, and for a moment thought he saw a second animal. He groaned and then fell unconscious.

Mike had seen a second dog. Happy was late arriving at the scene. She had plunged into the water and joined Wyn as she was nearing the shore with Mike in tow. She had swum beside them as though to honor Wyn's rescue. When they came out of the water, she investigated Mike's bleeding arm. She was aware of Wyn's feelings as she stood looking down at the body on the shore.

The sound from the man made Wyn stiffen and withdraw. The intensity of the rescue had passed. The powerful mandate of her ancestors had led to a moment of greatness. She had saved a human life. But now her old fears of man were surfacing again. She wanted to run away.

Her curious companion sniffed over Mike's unconscious body. She was still investigating when she looked up to see Wyn trotting off down the beach. When she saw Wyn head up the slope and disappear, Happy galloped after her.

Wyn stopped only once to look back toward the lake

below. Afternoon shadows stretched across the water. The sun striking the orange tent set it aglow. The man on the shore still had not moved. Happy followed Wyn up the narrow trail and over the ridge. Unwittingly, the two dogs retraced Mike's journey to the lake. They were heading home.

TWENTY-ONE

HOPE

Chuck sat in the den, relaxed in his big recliner, half-dozing, half-listening to the eleven o'clock news. He was waiting for the weather report. It was rare that Santa Anas lasted more than three days, and he was hoping for a break in the heat. He usually didn't stay up so late, but he was reluctant to head upstairs to the hot bedroom. When the weatherman finally appeared, he droned on about upper air currents and high pressure and the possibility of lower temperatures within thirty-six hours.

Getting up to turn off the set, Chuck called to Ann, "I'm turning in."

"Okay," she responded from the next room, "I'll be up in about half an hour."

Chuck reached for the television, but paused as the newscaster's words caught his attention. "Our final story tonight is an incredible one," she began. "A young backpacker returned to town today with an unbelievable account of how his life was saved—by a huge black animal!

"Mike Mortell, a native of San Diego, was hiking alone in the Lagunas, when he decided to beat the heat by swimming across Emerald Lake. But about halfway out, he realized he needed help."

Mike Mortell appeared on the screen.

"I was in serious trouble," he said. "The air was so warm, but the lake was a lot colder than I expected and I got real tired real quick."

"I tried to make it back to shore, but my body went numb. I literally could not move my arms and legs. And I thought, 'This is it. I'm going to die.' "

"Then out of nowhere I saw this huge black animal coming straight for me. It was making strange noises, I could hear as it got closer. I thought it was a bear, so I tried to push it away. But it kept circling me, and finally it just grabbed my arm and pulled me in."

The camera zoomed in on Mike's bruised arm.

"That animal saved my life," he said.

The screen switched back to the smiling newscaster. "Do you suppose bears have taken on lifeguard duty in our mountains?" she quipped.

Chuck stood up. He was stunned by the broadcast. His hand was still resting on the television set, his mind racing to process what he had heard. He knew full well the lifesaver was no bear. He was positive it was a large dog, and, barely able to believe such an incredible coincidence, he realized it might be Wyn or Happy!

He turned off the set and walked into the study where

Ann sat working at her desk. She was poring over pedigrees, studying a pair of young female Newfoundlands. If her research satisfied her, she hoped to buy one of the dogs. Chuck looked at his wife in the soft yellow lamplight. Losing Happy and Wyn had been devastating to her. Only recently had she accepted the idea that they were never coming back. Life had been easier since she'd begun looking ahead. He didn't want to stir up the old agony again, on the basis of false hopes.

Chuck, himself, could hardly stand to remember Ann's pain after the two dogs disappeared. She'd spent frustrating weeks searching, advertising, answering fruitless leads. To this day, she had no idea what had happened to her treasured animals.

"That's the hardest part," she'd said one day, "not knowing . . . " Her voice had trailed away into a whisper just short of tears.

Tormented with indecision, Chuck stood silently until she realized he was there and looked up. His strained expression frightened her. She got up and went to him. "Are you sick, honey?" she asked.

"No. No, I'm fine," he said. He took her by the shoulders and looked squarely at her. In that moment he knew what he must do.

"Come sit down, Ann. I have something to tell you," he said softly.

Ann rarely saw him in such a serious mood. She sat and listened to him quietly. The impact of the news left her without words. No emotion showed on her face, no indication of joy or hope or even disbelief. Chuck waited patiently for her reaction. It seemed an eternity before she spoke.

Slowly, she drew in a deep breath as if reliving the agony of the past year. Finally she spoke, "I'd like to go for a walk." She got up and looked at her husband. "I need you to come along," she said. "Please?"

Ann walked out to the patio where her big male Newfoundland lay sleeping. "Come on, Knight," she said. "Let's go for a walk." Her fingers ran deeply through his coat along his spine and up to his neck as she encouraged him out of his drowsiness. His tail wagged his response as he got up and shook off his sleepiness. Ann looked at Chuck again. "I think I'm afraid of hope," she admitted in a monotone, "but I believe there is a reason to hope . . . " Then she added, "I really need to go for a walk."

They walked over a mile in complete silence. The warm evening was quiet and peaceful in the neighborhood. There was no traffic, only the whooing sounds of owls calling softly to one another in the darkness.

Ann's thoughts were disjointed. She felt again the emptiness left by Happy's and Wyn's disappearance. She remembered being so distraught she could barely speak or move. For months, not knowing where they were, she had lived each day in frustration and torment. The longer they were gone from her, the more grim the possibilities were that came clearly to her mind, terrible thoughts of starvation, injury, even death.

And now this incredible news. Could it be Wyn? Or Happy? Was it really possible that one of them might have survived out there all these months? How? Where? And if so, which one? Where was the other?

As Ann thought of the incredible hardship that life in

the wild would be for a domestic animal, she contented herself with the thought that if the story were true, the animal had to be in good condition to respond so powerfully. But how would they find out the truth? Where should they call? What was the young man's name? Suddenly, Ann broke the silence of their walk with a flood of decisions. "It could have be one of them, Chuck. But even if it isn't, I've have to find out."

"I'm with you all the way, honey," Chuck said reassuringly. He tucked his arm around her waist and held her close as they headed toward home. He could feel her anticipation. It was like having her back again, he thought, after losing her for a long time. Even Knight seemed caught up in the contagious spirit of the moment. He trotted along beside them with an extra bounce to his step.

As they walked home, Chuck and Ann outlined the steps they should take. All the while as they planned, both minds knew this wild story offered only an obscure chance of finding Happy or Wyn. But both hearts yearned for it to be a reality.

TWENTY-TWO

SILVER COMMUNICATOR

Ann stared at the seeping wounds from teeth marks and the deep purple bruises on Mike's upper arm. She was amazed just looking at the wounds and thinking about the drama as it must have unfolded just three days ago. The purple stripes on his chest and legs were a familiar sight to her, for she, too, had been raked by powerful paws, during water training with her dogs.

Listening to Mike recount his story, Ann and Chuck sat spellbound. Each word rang true. They could visualize the beauty of the lake. They understood his feeling of oneness with the nature. It pained Ann to hear him describe the brown eyes locked on him, the groans of the rescuing animal as he continually struggled to escape. She understood the unrelenting need that pulsed within animals born to save lives. The story drew her emotionally closer to her dogs than she had felt in many

281

months. She realized they needed to move ahead quickly with their plans to return to the scene of the rescue.

It took two days of planning before they could begin their trek. Two endless days of rearranging schedules, assembling equipment, and making all the necessary last minute details. She felt frustrated at the amount of time it took to make appropriate plans. She was impatient to leave for Emerald Lake.

Mike agreed to help them retrace his route to the lake. They had to assume the lake was the animal's territory, and that it would remain in the area. They studied the map one last time and double-checked the list of equipment each would be carrying. One of Mike's friends agreed to drive them as far as he could up the mountain in his four-wheel drive truck. This boost would save time and energy.

At the drop-off point, Chuck watched his wife as she readjusted the equipment strapped to her pack. What if the search were unsuccessful? He would hurt for her. Still, they had only one choice. He would not deny her the opportunity to explore this possibility. Watching her pursue every report, every call, every lead when the dogs first disappeared, he had learned she would not rest until every clue was investigated. And deep inside, he, too, believed Mike's rescuer really could be one of their dogs. Motivated by that deep conviction, Chuck was ready to set out.

Ann stood staring down at her equipment. Tears welled in her eyes, blurring the backpack into meaningless patterns. "Oh God," she whispered. "Guide us safely to our goal." A tear splashed onto the pack and sparkled in the midday sun. Ann collected her emotions and went on with her equipment check. It felt good to have a sense of true purpose. Here she stood on the brink of an adventure that might lead her to Wyn or Happy. She took a deep breath and exhaled slowly. The fresh mountain air was invigorating. She picked up her pack and turned to Chuck for assistance in shouldering her load.

The three hikers exchanged little conversation as they began their climb. Mike led the way, enjoying his return to the mountains. He was anxious to see the sparkling beauty of Emerald Lake once more. Behind Mike, Chuck focused on methodically covering every angle in their attempt to locate the animal. Ann was glad for the silence, broken only by the sounds of their footsteps on the rugged trail.

A whistle hung around her neck on a leather thong. She had used it in training both dogs in the ocean breakers. Its shrill sound carried better than any voice could. Perhaps it would reach them now, if they were out here. Each time they rested, Ann blew three long whistle blasts, then watched and listened carefully for a response. There was none, but at least she was doing something!

They crested the steep slope, wound along the side, and then make their way down the north boundary of the lake to Mike's old campsite.

All three dropped their packs and began searching the area for any clues the black animal might have left behind. But they found nothing, not even a footprint. Ann's spirits sank. It was here, by the shore, that she'd hoped to see the first real clues.

Anticipation was the mood as the hikers set up their tents and rested by the lake. Except for the seriousness of their mission, it was a lovely evening. Once again, Mike went over his account of the rescue. He pointed out the route he had taken to the beach, where he'd entered the water, and where he had been dragged to shore.

"That way." He waved across the water. "I swam that way, and I ended up over there just below that ledge."

The Santa Ana conditions had finally subsided, and the night was actually cold. But that was not why Ann had trouble sleeping. She unzipped the flap on the tent and looked up at the night sky. It was filled with stars.

"You forgot how many stars there are when you live near the city," she said to Chuck. "They're so beautiful."

Ann struggled to recall the names of various clusters . . . Orion the Hunter, Taurus the Bull, the Pleiades, the Seven Sisters. Under the sky's immense expanse, she suddenly realized the insignificance of her quest within a greater plan. Still, she couldn't help wonder if any of the stars she saw were shining down on Wyn or Happy, somewhere on this mountain.

"Where are you?" she thought. "Where are you?" With a feeling of frustration, she turned her face away from the silent heavens.

Ann awoke shortly after daylight. She listened quietly, hoping for the sound of dogs splashing in the water or romping on the beach. But only the call of ravens in the tree tops broke the morning silence. There was a

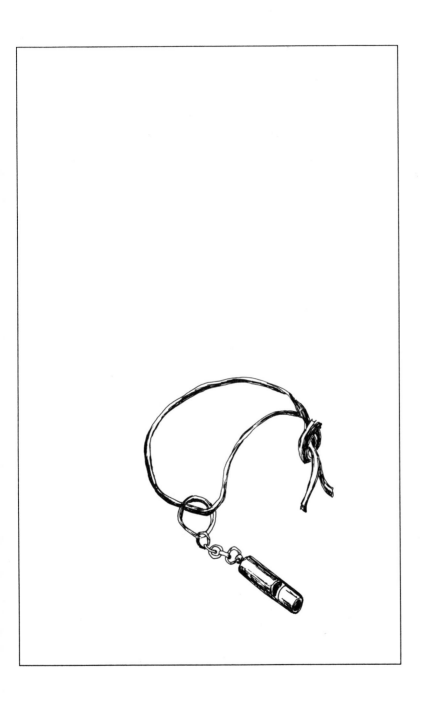

sense of urgency as the trio finished breakfast. The men studied their maps, pinpointing other nearby areas where water was available. They decided to travel north and east. The width of the valley in that direction would allow sounds to carry farther. Before they broke camp, Ann blew the whistle again three times. Again, nothing.

As they left the site, Mike stopped and looked back at the lake, still visible through the trees. "I had an eerie feeling the animal would come to the lake while we were there," he said to Ann. "But once we set up camp yesterday, I just had this funny feeling of emptiness." He shook his head. "Now, why would I feel like that? I know it was there, because it saved my life." With a shrug, Mike turned away from Emerald Lake and turned toward the sprawling valley beyond.

After all the months of disappointment, something within Ann would not let her believe completely that Mike's rescuer was one of her dogs. In fact, with each hour she became more convinced it was not her dog that saved Mike. Hers would have responded to the whistle.

Ann had the uneasy feeling time was nearly up. All day, they had explored the territory thoroughly without any sign of a dog. They'd met only one hiker, who hadn't seen or heard a dog either. Maybe it was time to give up. But something had carried Mike to shore. What was it? Why couldn't they find it?

Late afternoon, they set up camp on a ridge overlooking the valley. Around the campfire, they began to talk of leaving the mountain.

In desperation, Ann blew the whistle again and again, then listened, as always, for a responding bark or the rustle of an animal rushing headlong through the brush. But all she heard was the yelping of coyotes. In the darkness, the tiny campfire flickered like a smoldering hope, unwilling to die.

Wyn didn't really know exactly what had awakened her, but a sound had penetrated her sleep and jolted her to her feet. Her ears twitched and shifted as she waited to hear it again, but it never came. Still, Wyn felt restless now. She paced for a long time before lying down again.

Happy could sense her friend's uneasiness. She watched her for a while, but gradually relaxed into an easy sleep.

"It's getting late, Ann," Chuck said. "How about a cup of fresh coffee before you turn in?" He held out a steaming cup. Ann took it gratefully, smiling a thank you. She drank slowly, staring out into the darkness at the faint outline of mountains against a blue-black sky. She sighed deeply, put the whistle to her lips for the last time that night and then the silver communicator was silent. The conversation behind her dropped off as all three campers waited for a response. But again there was none. Ann turned back to the camp circle. She could feel the men's eyes as she washed her cup, shook it and hung it on a branch for morning. She smiled at the two of them, said good night, and crawled into her tent.

Wyn was awake and listening this time when the whistle pierced the darkness. Immediately, she recognized the sound. It was a sound from her past, a call to come. Still conditioned by her early training, she quivered. The torment of her loneliness for one special person seemed intensified by the whistle call. It tugged at her like a magnet. Leaving Happy asleep, she slipped off into the darkness toward the compelling sound.

Wyn stopped occasionally to listen, then resumed her journey, moving unerringly in the right direction. She did not hear the whistle again, but its sound was still ringing in her ears, beckoning to her through the darkness. Soon, she could hear voices, men's voices.

Cautiously now, Wyn moved close enough to the voices to see the campfire. It reminded her of the recent scare at another campfire. Remembering the screaming woman and the raging man, Wyn sniffed for information about these humans. Despite her reservations, she was drawn closer to them by the thought of the whistle.

Chuck poked slowly and deliberately at the fire with a stick. Mike had fetched a bucket of water from a stream to douse the last embers, but he set it aside and sat down again. Both men felt reluctant to leave the warmth and pleasure of the dying flames. Suddenly, Chuck caught a glimpse of a shadowy figure just beyond the firelight. Involuntarily, he moved toward it, but it vanished into the forest.

"Mike, did you see something?" Chuck whispered. "Over there, just beyond the big tree?" Mike shook his head and shaded his face from the campfire, hoping for a better look. "I only saw it for a second," Chuck continued. "It was acting wild and spooky, but it looked pretty big."

United in a single thought, the men exchanged an intense glance. Chuck added some wood to the fire, hoping for better light, then each searched the darkness again, straining for another glimpse of their visitor.

They were at once hopeful that the creature would return, but at the same time wondering if it might not be one of the dogs at all, but instead a wild animal. They knew bears were not common in these mountains, but they'd discussed reports of occasional mountain lion sightings in the area.

Suddenly, the animal moved out of the shadows again and into the firelight's outer edge. The flickering light reflected in its eyes. By now, Chuck had seen enough to convince himself that it was a dog, and a pretty good-sized one. Still, it was too far away in the darkness to see any detail. Both men could sense the animal's fear. Chuck spoke softly in its direction, but it disappeared again. They heard the crackle of a few broken twigs, then silence.

Without moving, Chuck whispered toward the tent. "Ann! Ann, get up!" He waited a moment, than spoke again. "We have company, and I believe it's a dog. Ann? Are you awake?"

"Yes, yes! I'm coming," Ann whispered back.

"It's been here about ten minutes," Chuck explained. "It's just hanging around out there in the darkness. It's real skittish. It disappeared when I moved, came back, then disappeared again when I spoke to it."

Chuck's words flooded Ann's mind as she rushed to dress in the confines of the little tent. Her feelings ran from panic to calm, from urgency to control, all in a few moments. Her hands were shaking as she tried to lace her boots. After what seemed hours, she crawled through the tent opening.

"Honey, it's big," Chuck said as she joined him by

the fire. "And I'm pretty sure it's black. It could be a Newf." He gestured with a stick in the direction of the animal. Then he leaned over and put another piece of wood on the fire.

Ann could feel her heart pounding as she walked slowly to the edge of the campsite and then stopped to listen. She heard the crack of a twig and realized with a thrill that something was out there in the darkness. It hurt to hope so much. She had to know. With tears slipping down her cheeks, Ann called softly into the darkness. "Here girl . . . are you out there?" Trembling, she sank to her knees and stretched out her arms. "Come on, girl." Her voice grew stronger. "Here girl, come here!"

Drawn by the familiar voice, but still cautious, Wyn edged forward through the darkness until she caught the scent of the kneeling woman. It was the right scent, so familiar and so much a part of her life. She stepped into full view.

Ann caught her breath as she took in the scene, lighted by the campfire . . . big head and broad muzzle, the dear familiar face. This was her dog! This was Wyn, materializing like a miracle out of the darkness!

"Oh, Chuck!" Ann cried, choking with tears and laughter. "It's Wyn! It's Wyn! It's really Wyn!"

Wyn moved steadily forward, closer and closer to her human. Finally, her nose touched Ann's outstretched hand, and an eery sound erupted from deep within the dog, unleashing all the pain and loneliness of the past months. Ann had never heard that sound come from a dog before, and she would never hear it again. She remained motionless. "Good girl . . . good girl," she soothed as Wyn sniffed over her face and hair and eyes. Then Wyn's tail began to wag. The more she sniffed, the more it wagged. These were familiar smells! Familiar hair. Familiar skin. A composite of everything she had longed for was here in this one person. Wyn's muzzle traveled over Ann's whole body until she felt sure that indeed this was her human. Then sniffing gave way to licking and whining, and finally to groans of joy as the big animal pressed herself into Ann's arms.

Ann dug deep into the thick coat as she held Wyn close to her in a long embrace. Then with both hands she began stroking Wyn's head, down her neck, over her back and down her sides.

"She's bigger," Ann thought. "Much bigger than I remember." "She's all muscle!" she said out loud. "Good heavens, she's solid." Overwhelmed, Ann buried her face in Wyn's shoulder and sobbed out her joy and relief. "Thank you God," she whispered.

After a long time, Ann broke away and turned toward the men at the campfire. The intensity of the reunion they had just witnessed meant something very different to Chuck and Mike, yet tears glistened on both their faces.

Now Wyn greeted each of them lavishly, stumbling over them with her big feet and washing their tears away with her big pink tongue. All fear was gone from her. Her trusting nature had been restored simply by the touch of the right human. The forest echoed with the sounds of celebration: laughter, tears, and laughter again.

Finally, the campsite quieted. Wyn curled up at Ann's feet. Mike stood and gazed down at the huge black dog. He was alive because of her. He did not speak, but knelt beside her and placed his hands on her shoulders, as if to confirm to himself that she was real and not just a dream. He did not share his thoughts or feelings, but nodded toward Ann and Chuck, then disappeared into the privacy of his orange tent.

Chuck and Ann sat for a long time in silence. At last, Chuck gave Ann a hug, "I am so happy for you," he whispered. And with a sigh, he lifted himself wearily from the fireside. He smiled at Ann as he reminded her to douse the fire. Then he, too, turned in for the night.

The rekindled fire again burned low. Ann sat close to her Newfoundland with one arm tucked around Wyn's deep chest. The dog's head rested on Ann's leg. Neither of them moved. Ann watched in complete contentment as the little fire dwindled to a few red coals. She didn't try to think of Wyn's past months or the challenge she had met in Emerald Lake. For the moment, just having her dog beside her again was all that she could ask.

As the fire died, Ann could feel the cold. She pulled herself away from Wyn and retrieved her sleeping bag from the tent. With Ann's first motion, Wyn was awake. Attentively, she followed Ann's every step as she spread the sleeping bag out under the stars and dutifully put out the remaining fire, watering and stirring the ashes until the last red ember hissed away into darkness. Then Ann crawled into her snug bag and zipped out the chill. One arm reached out in the darkness, fell on Wyn's coat and moved with it as the dog circled close to Ann's body and lay down.

Wyn awakened frequently during the night, still joyful in the realization that Ann was nearby. She walked heavily on the sleeping bag and searched under its covers. She snuffled at Ann's head and face, inhaling the familiar scent, then sneezed and snuffled some more. Finally assured of Ann's presence, the big dog settled down to sleep again.

Like Wyn, Ann slept very little. A million thoughts still churned in her mind with one stark reality . . . only one dog had come back.

TWENTY-THREE

PEACE

Happy lifted her head and looked around. The first light of a new day appeared in the eastern sky. Happy could see and sense that Wyn was gone. She listened for any sound of Wyn in the area near their sleeping quarters. She heard nothing. The pair had been constant companions since they had left Will. Now, Happy felt very much alone, and the feeling brought her to her feet. An intense need to find her friend churned within her. So with her nose to the ground in search of scent, Happy made a wide circle through the area.

It was easy to pick up Wyn's trail and follow it down the hillside and across the dry creek bed, and accurately determine where Wyn had begun her climb up the other side of the valley. At times the forest was thick and difficult to get through, but Happy persistently trailed after her friend. As the day became brighter, she continued to close the gap between them. She was not drawn by the same need to find Ann or by the shrill and compelling lure of the whistle. Happy merely wanted to be with her companion.

The camp on the ridge was a hub of activity. All three campers were busy striking their tents, packing up cooking gear, assembling their packs, and preparing for the return home. Wyn mingled with them as they worked, occasionally getting in the way, and frequently receiving a firm pat or gentle word just for being near. Each spoke to the dog as though she could understand every word.

They finished packing, then they took time out for a ceremonial last cup of coffee before they began their journey down the mountain. It was a bittersweet time for each as they sat together in an experience that could never be repeated. Wyn lay close to Ann's feet wagging her tail occasionally, looking up and leaning toward her for an extra pat. There was an air of quiet jubilation in camp.

They compared the bruises on Mike's arm with Wyn's mouth and came to the unshakable conclusion that Wyn had indeed saved him from drowning in the lake. Ann told Mike a few of the confirmed stories she knew about the powerful rescue instincts carried in some Newfoundland dogs.

Suddenly, Wyn swung her head around to face the forest trail, her ears alert. Her move alerted the others. All eyes followed her line of vision as she watched, aware of things the humans were not able to sense.

No one spoke. Each was curious about what Wyn had heard. Each expected to see a hiker come into view.

Wyn stood up, then she moved to the edge of the clearing still intent on the sound from the forest. The humans could hear sounds now, too. Wyn moved a step or two closer, then stopped, her head up. Her tail began to wag lightly.

Happy had finished her climb up the steep slope and made her way through the brush and into the clearing. She trotted up to Wyn. They touched muzzles in their usual greeting and celebrated their reunion with a few playful gestures. Then Happy moved to greet the astonished humans, first Ann, then Chuck, and then the stranger.

Mike stood and stared at Happy. A moment of the rescue flashed in his mind. He spoke, almost to himself. "Now that I think about it, there were two dogs!" He paused, then continued. "I thought I was hallucinating, but I did see two animals when I was dragged up on the shore." He had mentioned it only briefly and put it out of his mind.

Not even Ann had given serious thought to the fact that Happy might still be alive, and with Wyn. She fell to her knees and engulfed the second dog. There was a small scar on Happy's side, not nearly as obvious as the one Wyn would wear on her shoulder forever. The dog was in good condition. Her body was well muscled and hard. She was heavier and had matured handsomely. Even after all the months away, she was a beautiful dog. Numbly, Ann said, "She's . . . she's fine. She's just fine." Then she stood and looked down at Happy. "I just don't believe what I'm seeing. I don't believe this could really happen. It's a miracle they could survive out here all alone for so long."

299

No one said much. Each just stared in wonder at the pair of dogs mingling happily with the humans. Ann put the little camp stove away. Each tucked away his coffee cup and shouldered a pack. "I want to go home," she said softly, almost wearily. "I can hardly wait to get home."

★ ★ ★ ★ ★

On another mountain, far to the south, a young male pup restlessly paced and explored every inch of the inside of Will's cabin. Interesting scents lured him. Sometimes, he even found little bits of food that Will had purposely left for him to discover.

All the while, Will sat very still, watching. When the pup had satisfied his curiosity, he went to the closed door and scratched. Will did not move. At last, the pup lay down at the closed door, and slept. This was the first night in his new home.

Will smiled.

★ ★ ★ ★ ★

Wyn and Happy responded to the reunion with the big male with great enthusiasm. He stood with patient dignity as the girls sniffed and nudged him, then he examined them as if they were strangers in his territory. He had not forgotten them. His memory jostled by their scents, his casual demeanor melted away to near puppy exuberance as he welcomed them back into his world. Together, they raced through the tropical plants and up and down the steep banks of their home. The females were more than a match for the old male as they tested each other's strength. Panting heavily, the male soon sidelined himself, joining Ann and Chuck on the patio while the girls continued to expend their energies in jubilant play and exploration. They were home!

The sun set. Darkness spread across the yard. It had been a day full of emotion for Ann as well as her New-foundlands. She stood at the patio door, looking at the two dogs sprawled on the lawn. They were stretched full length in complete relaxation. She was drawn to them, to touch them, to be sure they really were here, and this was not a dream.

As she approached the mounded figures, Wyn's head popped up. She was not sleeping. She was simply at peace with her surroundings. She offered a welcome tail wag as Ann found a place on the grass next to her warmth. Happy joined them, circled, and lay down close enough to touch. Ann's hand ran through their luxuriant coats, feeling the hard-muscled bodies, sa-voring their presence. Once again, reality grabbed her. Here she was. One wonderful friend at each side to reach out and touch. They were home!

Ann sat on the grass with Wyn and Happy for a while. When she moved to get up, she realized how weary she was. Neither dog moved as she extricated herself from their warmth and quietly made her way back to the house. As she slid the patio door closed, she realized that she had given no thought to where they would sleep, or want to sleep. Inside? Out in the open as they had for many months? After only a moment hesitation, she reopened the sliding door, just enough to permit an interested Newfoundland to enter. The cool air rushed in. The damp, fragrant air was sweet in her nostrils. She looked out at the two still forms on her lawn. With a smile, she turned away from the open door and went to bed.

The dense fog swept in silently and enveloped Happy and Wyn. Moisture collected on their black coats and on everything around them. A frog chirruped his call and it blended with the sounds of moisture dripping from the acacia and eucalyptus. Muffled by the fog, a coyote call drifted to Wyn's ears. She lifted her head and listened. It was not her coyote. She sniffed the sweet smells of home, listened to the gentle sounds of dripping moisture. The frog chirruped again.

Wyn stood and shook, waking Happy. They touched noses in the darkness, then together made their way to the open doorway. Ann heard their thumping approach on the stairs. With a smile, she waited. She could hear them sniffing their way through the bedroom, making their way around the sleeping male who was camped on the floor at the foot of the bed. More snuffling, then Wyn greeted her with a large wet muzzle pushing its way into the covers. Sniffing her human, the dog expressed her joy with whines and exuberant tail-wagging.

Happy forced herself between Wyn and the bed to offer her own expression of happiness. After a brief moment of reassurance that Ann and Chuck were both there, Happy flopped down near the big male.

Wyn's body was still vibrating with tails wags as she gave Ann a final good night kiss with the tip of her tongue. Then she circled into just the right space, with her back pressed lightly against Ann's side of the bed, and folded into her chosen sleeping place.

Ann reached down in the darkness and touched her dog. She could feel the ribcage rise and fall with each breath. Wyn's warmth was comforting.

Through the open bedroom windows came the sounds of the chaparral night. The little frog sang his winter song; a coyote signaled to his pack from the far hillside.

Wyn listened. Aware of Ann's hand still resting gently on her side, she stretched full length. She was home. Her restless and lonely search was over. She wagged her tail just once more, then drifted into a deep and peaceful slumber.

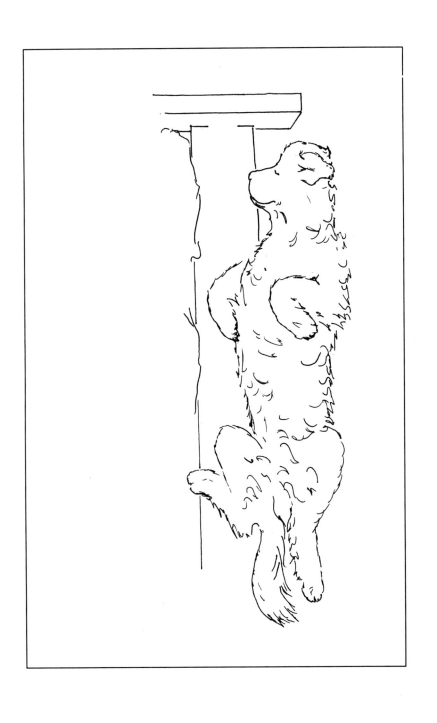